St. Thom

D1091393

THE WINE OF ETERNITY · SHORT STORIES FROM THE LATVIAN

TRANSLATED BY RUTH SPEIRS AND HARALDS KUNDZINS

THE WINE OF ETERNITY

Short Stories from the Latvian

BY KNUTS LESINS

UNIVERSITY OF MINNESOTA PRESS

© Copyright 1957 by the University of Minnesota

Printed at the North Central Publishing Co., St. Paul

Library of Congress Catalog Card Number: 57-13117

PUBLISHED IN GREAT BRITAIN, INDIA, AND PAKISTAN BY THE
OXFORD UNIVERSITY PRESS, LONDON, BOMBAY, AND KARACHI

The decorative devices used throughout are adapted from
typical Latvian property marks

ABOUT THE AUTHOR

KNUTS LESINS was born in 1909, of Latvian parents. His father came from a farming family, his mother's people were townsfolk. Both parents had various interests: his father wrote a few novels, played the violin, and was greatly interested in philosophy and music; his mother taught foreign languages, translated books, sang, and played the piano. Thus he grew up in a lively, stimulating atmosphere and developed the two interests which have lasted all his life — literature and music.

He studied the piano at the Latvian State Conservatory, Riga, and graduated in 1932 with an M.A. degree in music. He developed a great interest in the history of music and composition, and he has written about twenty solo songs, preludes, and other compositions. For many years he taught at the State School of Music, and for seven years he held the post of Assistant Director (Dramatist) at the Latvian National Opera in Riga. He took part in many concerts as soloist and accompanist, and worked for the Riga broadcasting station as a lecturer and commentator on musical events.

Along with his interest in music — which he shares with his wife Valda, a singer — he has always been interested in literature, and he has read widely in the German, Russian, French, and English classics. While still a student, he wrote a spate of youthfully romantic

v

poems which gathered dust in various editors' desks. Then he tried his hand at writing short stories. In 1929 one of them was accepted for publication, and from then onwards his work was much published in Latvia.

When straitened financial circumstances, owing to the death of his father, forced Lesins to discontinue his law studies — which he had taken up in order to learn a useful profession in case all else failed — he worked as a journalist and as a literary and art critic for various Latvian papers. In his capacity as a journalist he traveled in the Scandinavian countries and visited many places in both the East and West of Europe.

He continued writing short stories, and in 1938 the first volume of collected short stories, *Omens in the Dark*, appeared, to be followed by *Faces and Problems in Latvian Music* (essays) in 1939, and by his first novel, *The Seal of Love*, in 1943.

He left Latvia in 1944 when the Russians invaded his country for the second time. He had made a name for himself, he had put down firm roots, he had become established in the Latvian literary world — and suddenly he had to start life all over again, first in Germany, and then in the United States where he has been living since 1950, working as a piano instructor. But he never gave up writing; eight more volumes of his work have so far been published by Latvian publishers in Germany and Sweden: *Reflections* (short stories), 1946; *Things That Arrange Themselves* (humorous short stories), 1948; *The Wine of Eternity* (short stories), 1949; *John the Musician* (novel), 1950; *The Proud Hearts* (short stories), 1952; *Dead End Street* (short stories), 1955; *Under Foreign Stars* (sketches, reminiscences), 1956; and *The Last Home* (novel), 1957. The present book is the first to appear in English, and contains translations of selections from the volumes listed above as well as other stories.

Knuts Lesins studied and worked in town — in Riga, the capital of Latvia — but he had not always lived there, and his love for his native countryside went very deep. I might mention one particular period in his life, the years 1922–27, when his father, after working at the Ministry of Agriculture, had obtained a post in connection with the agrarian reform. The family spent those five years on a small estate near the town of Valmiera, in a very lovely part of the country, close to the river Gauja. In reminiscences written in 1947, Lesins describes that period of his boyhood in such loving detail that one almost sees every tree, every stone at the bottom of the river, every fish, every ripple on the water. His love for the Latvian countryside is a very real thing. Coupled with it is his understanding of the Latvian countryfolk, their lavish, stubborn hospitality ("The Fiery Descent of Old Koris"), their pride ("In the Blizzard"), their shrewd humor and buffoonery in the face of danger ("The Tailor and the Wolves"), and their dark, tragic entanglements ("The Secret," "A String of Beads").

He belongs to the generation of Latvian writers who, during their childhood, witnessed their country's struggle for independence. When the new state was born there was a creative upsurge in the various fields of the arts; the young writers were full of new ideas, and new trends developed in literature. Then everything was cut short by the events of the Second World War. Latvia was — and still is — occupied by Russia, and a large number of Latvian authors went into exile. It is a very difficult thing to start life again from the beginning, and one requires great inner resources to do it. Lesins has these resources. In all his writing since the tragic debacle overtook his country there is no hint of bitterness, of accusation, of self-pity. His dominant interest is in human values; even though man is vulnerable and subject to the uncertainties of fate, he prefers his precarious existence to a condition of "happy nonexistence" ("One-Day Land").

Throughout his writing, Lesins preserves an endearingly calm wisdom and humanity, an imperturbable spirit, kindly humor, and a quiet charm. It is this quietness which makes his work seem deceptively slight at the first reading; he does not use big words, he is not spectacular, he does not preach or propound. He sits back and observes. He observes ordinary, everyday people, but his understanding of humanity and human situations is such that even the simplest character in his stories has a completeness, and therefore a kind of beauty, which another writer might not have achieved. This completeness has been remarked by Janis Andrups, a Latvian critic, who says: "Lesins has no pretensions towards presenting a large panorama of life; he presents episodes and momentary glimpses which yet reveal the whole — the whole man, the completeness of life."

He often places his characters in situations where they have to make instantaneous decisions, alone, with no help or advice from outside. Although these decisions may sometimes seem paradoxical ("In the Blizzard") they are natural and logical to the person concerned because they are anchored in all that makes him what he is. Sometimes the process goes further, and the decision made by a very ordinary man raises him to a higher plane, leading him to the fulfilment of his destiny ("The Dove").

We have seen that Knuts Lesins has, on his father's side, generations of farmers behind him. Farmers must be patient and calm in all calamities that might befall their crops, their livestock, their very existence. The Latvian farmer and peasant in particular has centuries of patient endurance behind him — for centuries he has had to live under foreign overlords. Yet he has preserved his language, his customs, his songs, his individuality. In the same way, Lesins, calm and patient, has remained true to himself.

He draws his strength from a tranquil acceptance of life and the conviction that everything in it has meaning and purpose. He does not try to force his views upon anybody; he leaves it to the reader to stop and think for himself.

Ruth Speirs

LATVIA AND ITS PEOPLE

ALTHOUGH most of these short stories deal with modern times and universal psychological problems, they reflect also certain peculiarities of the history and life of the Latvian people. So it seemed advisable to the writer to tell something about his country, its background and customs.

Latvia won its independence from Russia after the First World War in a struggle which united five nations — Latvia, Estonia, Lithuania, Finland, and Poland — in a common striving for freedom. Thus Europe was provided with a so-called *cordon sanitaire* against communism, and the first experiment in "peaceful coexistence" was started. The experiment ended with Soviet Russia taking over all of those countries except Finland. As historians point out, the problem of the Baltic countries (Latvia, Estonia, and Lithuania) was not the result of either the First or the Second World War. Their territory has long been the key to the domination of the Baltic Sea. That is why Peter the Great, the grandfather of Russian imperialism, proclaimed: "I am interested in the sea, not in the land." In occupying the Baltic states in 1940, his true disciple Stalin only followed his example.[1]

Latvia is situated on the eastern shore of the Baltic Sea, between

[1] Arveds Schwabe, *Histoire du peuple Letton*, Stockholm, 1953.

Estonia to the north and Lithuania to the south. Its area during its independence (1918–40), 25,402 square miles (about the size of West Virginia), consisted mostly of cultivated land, the rest being covered by forests and marshes. The population of Latvia during its independence numbered two million, of whom approximately 77 per cent were of Latvian ancestry. Seventy per cent of the population were Protestants, 27 per cent Roman Catholics, others Greek Orthodox and Jewish. Latvia's largest city is its capital, Riga, a seaport with 400,000 inhabitants. Riga is situated at the mouth of the river Daugava, which divides the country into two parts and has served as a route for trade from ancient times.

Latvia is an agricultural country and 65 per cent of its population in the interwar period was rural. The individual farm surrounded by orchards, beehives, and flower gardens was the characteristic feature of the landscape.

The Latvian people have a strong, resisting, quiet, and at the same time sensitive character. The land, being on the whole difficult to farm, calls for a people bound by a close spiritual unity, for lovers of seclusion, fully conscious that the only way to get a reward is by hard work.[2]

Like the now extinct Old Prussians, the Latvians and the Lithuanians have languages that are closer to the Sanskrit than is any other Indo-European language. The Estonians speak a Finno-Ugric language.

Toward the end of the twelfth century the Latvians were divided into three tribal kingdoms. The spreading of Christianity in the name of the Holy Roman Empire was undertaken in the early years of the thirteenth century by the Livonian Knights. Their methods of conquest and rule were so cruel that in 1222 Pope Honorius III threatened the order with interdict and excommunication should the Knights continue their brutalities. The warning was repeated in 1237 by Pope Gregory IX. In 1354 the papal delegate to Riga pro-

[2] Arnolds Spekke, *History of Latvia,* M. Goppers, Stockholm, 1951.

claimed interdict and excommunication of the Livonian order. However, this did not help, since the invaders were really interested not in the spreading of Christianity but in gaining power and wealth. The last to resist the invaders was the Latvian tribe of Zemgallians, which after its defeat, and considering its case as hopeless, emigrated en masse to Lithuania except for some members who were resettled in northern Latvia.

The struggle for the domination of the Baltic Sea went on between the Hanseatic League (a mercantile league of German towns), Denmark, Sweden, the Livonian order, Lithuania, Poland, and Russia. In 1561 the Duchy of Courland sprang up under Polish suzerainty in what is now western Latvia, enjoying a comparatively long period of independence and prosperity, building ships for the English kings, establishing colonies on the island of Tobago in the Atlantic Ocean near South America and in Gambia in West Africa. Tobago and Gambia later became parts of the British Empire, but some Latvian names are preserved there, as reminders of a peculiar period of history.

Sweden's domination of the Baltic, established by Gustavus II in the first half of the seventeenth century, lasted throughout that century, marking a period of enlightened and progressive rule. The records show that some stubborn Latvian peasants, oppressed by the landlords, sailed across the Baltic to present their pleas to the Swedish king. The policy of Swedish rulers at that time was to side with the peasants in order to gain more power against the local nobility.

Swedish rule was ended in the Northern War (1700–1721) by Peter the Great's devastating conquest and was followed by the rule of the Czars till the end of the Russian Empire and the establishment of the Free Republic of Latvia.

In the course of many centuries of foreign domination, broken only by short periods of freedom, the Latvian peasant learned to trust nobody but himself. He developed his folk art, his colorful national costume, the beauty and philosophy of his folk song and fairy-tale, and he succeeded in preserving his national character and his language.

The Latvian folk song is the most remarkable inheritance of the centuries of division by foreign rulers and continual wars and destruction.

> The bird is singing, brother sweet!
> He has been singing, loud and long.
> Go listen, sister and repeat
> To me the story of his song.
>
> I saw my brother in the fight.
> I saw him battling with his lord.
> With five bright bands his hat was dight,
> A sixth was waving from his sword!
>
> The field was strewed with men at rest,
> Hewn down like oaks. I saw the spear,
> The murderous spear in many a breast,
> And all was horrid silence there.

The English version is by Sir Walter Scott, published with some others in the *Foreign Quarterly Review* in 1831. The tendency of romanticism to have a closer look at the art of plain people was started by the English bishop Thomas Percy, whose work greatly impressed the German humanitarian writer Johann Herder, a teacher in Riga at this time. While visiting his friends in the country, Herder saw Latvian peasants celebrating their national feast, "Jani" (Jon's Day — Midsummer Eve), with all their customs, singing, and dancing. He asked some clergymen to send him samples of Latvian and Estonian folk songs and published them in German translation in an anthology in 1778. Pastor Gustav Bergmann, influenced by Herder's activity, published two more collections of Latvian folk songs. The English folklorist Jamson, who lived for some years in Riga and was acquainted with Bergmann, presented those collections to Sir Walter Scott, who was fascinated by the freshness of expression and folk philosophy.

But the immense task of collecting all the folk songs available and still sung by the people was accomplished by the Latvian Krisjanis Barons. He found his collaborators in every corner of the country, most of them enthusiastic schoolteachers. They went from farm to farm, writing down every verse known by elderly people. Barons spent forty years of his life collecting and classifying folk songs in eight volumes with 35,789 original songs and 182,000 variations. During Latvia's independence, Professor Peteris Smits continued Barons' work, publishing four more volumes and increasing the number of original songs to 60,000. Most of these songs are very short, consisting of only four lines.

Although the custom of singing everywhere, at home, at work, and on many social occasions, is gradually vanishing in the twentieth century, especially in the towns, choir singing has flourished since the middle of the last century and is a custom of Latvians in exile At the first General Song-Festival in 1873, in Riga, 55 selected choirs with 1,000 singers took part. This number increased to 16,-000 singers at the ninth General Song-Festival in 1938.

A schoolteacher and a writer, Ansis Lerchis-Puskaitis, collected Latvian fairytales and legends. His work, too, was completed by Professor Peteris Smits. Though the fairytales reflect the mood and customs of the Latvian people, they often have ancient universal themes that could have been borrowed by others and localized or could have been created by similar conditions and problems in distant lands.

The beginnings of Latvian writing can be traced to the medieval past. Simon Grunau in his *Prussian Chronicles*, written in about 1530, mentions that several old books in the language of the ancient Prussians, and even in peculiar Prussian characters, had been lost. As the Latvians and the ancient Prussians were Baltic peoples closely akin to each other and in the period up to the thirteenth century at about the same cultural level, we may presume that the Latvians, too, had characters of their own resembling neither the Latin nor the Gothic alphabet, but perhaps most akin to the Scandinavian runes. This presumption is supported by the fact that on some very old Latvian harps there are engraved signs resembling the runes.[3]

The Roman Catholic Church provided only religious texts and books in Latvian. The centuries from the thirteenth through the sixteenth were the flourishing age of folk song, because church services, performed in Latin, were not understood by the people. In the seventeenth century, when the Reformation swept the northern Baltic provinces, the Lutheran German Protestant Church started services in Latvian and all people sang hymns, translated often very awkwardly by pastors, who at the same time started fighting witches, pagan worship, old social customs, and folk songs. However, there were some men who devoted themselves to the studies of the Latvian language, publishing dictionaries, sermons, and in 1689 the Bible in a Latvian translation by Pastor E. Glück.

The Northern War, as noted, ended with the defeat of Sweden and the loss of its Baltic provinces to Russia. Destruction by war was followed by a plague which killed 60 per cent of the country people. In order to have some support from the nobility, Peter the Great guaranteed to the landlords all the privileges that had been reduced by Swedish rule, and in the course of time more were added. To the more enlightened landlords, serfdom, one of their "privileges", began to look not very profitable economically; others were influenced by true idealism. Thus in 1819 serfdom was abolished in Latvia, in such a way that the peasants were free to go where they pleased. But, having no land of their own, they found there was practically no place to go. False rumors circulated among the peasants that the Czar had granted some more rights to them but that the landlords were withholding the news. Some peasant revolts started. They were put down by the Russian military forces. The leaders were punished severely and some deported to Siberia. Some reminders of those events can be found in my story "The Tailor and the Wolves," while "The Wine of Eternity" is partially based on a

[3] Karlis Dzilleja, in *The New Word*, No. 2, 1946, Meerbeck, Germany.

Latvian fairytale and presents some samples of characteristic Latvian folk songs.

The use of folklore as a source of inspiration became common among many Latvian writers, especially during the period of so-called National Awakening (the second half of the nineteenth century), when the peasants were allowed to buy farms, more and more of them improved their standing in the cities as artisans, workers, and merchants, and many of them graduated from high schools and universities.

But the Czarist censors kept a sharp eye on every Latvian book and newspaper. This is why Latvian poets often used symbols to express their ideas of independence. The great Latvian poet Rainis developed a new kind of symbolic drama, reviving heroes from the ancient past (at least their names) or creating symbolic figures from his imagination, and writing his dialogues in the form of folk songs.

The linkage between the folklore and modern Latvian literature, however, was never quite complete. Poetry sometimes absorbed the mood and the spirit of the folk song, but at the same time developed the system of rhymes and meters that could be found in the classical, romantic, or modern poetry of other nations. In the same way the novel, the short story, and drama could not be developed fully from fairytales, but followed the usual trends of realism and human psychology. Thus Rudolfs Blaumanis, the first great master of Latvian short story and drama, has nothing in common with the romanticism of National Awakening, but is a realist with a deep knowledge of peasant life and human passion.

The problems, style, and the forms of Latvian literature, which is really only a hundred years old, vary according to the development of different aspects of the nation's life. So the greatest variety of forms and moods naturally started to flourish during Latvia's independence from 1918 to 1940. This is also reflected in some figures on book publishing. In those years, 22,000 Latvian books were published — twice the number brought out in the 333 years before.

There grew up a new generation of poets and writers who enjoyed freedom of expression. Some discussed Joyce, Proust, Gide, and Rilke, looking no more for national problems but for their own way. The mood and style of poetry and prose became more playful.

While the older generation grew up mostly with a thorough knowledge of Russian and German literature, the younger one during independence was more diversified and discriminating. The deep pessimism of Dostoyevsky and Chekhov and the pathetic morality of Tolstoy never appealed to the Latvian taste despite the country's history of subjugation. The communist constraint on writers, which made the modern Russian literature very low in quality, helped to accomplish the break from that literature. The German classics were still appreciated but now were regarded only as a link to Western literature. The short story writer Janis Ezerins (1891–1924) already showed the trend of following the Romance-language short story; the poet Wirza (1883–1940), with his masterly translations of French lyrics in two volumes, showed the ability to adapt verse forms of the Romance languages. On the other hand the tradition of Latvian peasant literature and folklore is still strong in the fairytales of Karlis Skalbe (1879–1945) and in the short short stories of Janis Jaunsudrabins (born in 1877), now living in Germany and the dean of Latvian writers. The poet Janis Medenis (born in 1903) made attempts at creating new Latvian meters by using longer lines than those customary in the folk song.

Never feeling quite at ease between their great neighbors, the Russians and Germans, the Latvians tried to strengthen all kinds of cultural intercourse with the West and Scandinavia. The establishing of the French Lyceum and the English Institute in Riga helped this trend. There were some older political influences, too. Karlis Ulmanis, later to become the first prime minister of Latvia, spent some years in exile in the United States after the unsuccessful revolution against the Czar in 1905, graduating from the University of Nebraska. At the same time the poet Rainis lived in Switzerland, returning to independent Latvia only in 1920. Of others who had emigrated to Western Europe, Norway, and the United States, in order to escape exile in Siberia, many never returned, but some preserved their attachment and connections to their native country. Between 1919 and 1925, 220,000 refugees returned to free Latvia.

With the goal of strengthening the Latvian economy and to provide a resistance to communistic tendencies the Latvian government in 1920 embarked on large-scale agrarian reform. The old-established holdings of the small farmer, which were the backbone of the national renaissance in the nineteenth century, were not touched, but all the big estates were distributed among the war veterans and landless peasants as small farms, sufficient to provide a living for a family. This created social content and economic prosperity which not only satisfied domestic needs, but also provided the basis of the export trade.

There were also remarkable achievements in education and culture. At the beginning of 1920 there were only 864 elementary schools, but at the end of 1933 there were 2,057. The six years of the elementary school were free and compulsory. The University of Riga in 1939, on its twentieth anniversary, had 446 professors and 7,247 students. Latvian scholars started to explore the Latvian language, literature, art, history, and law, using foreign and local sources and archives which had been neglected in the past. The Latvian Conservatoire and the Latvian Academy of Arts provided facilities for higher education in music and painting. The Latvian National Opera was well known in Europe through its opera productions, its soloists, and its ballet.

The world economic crisis which began in 1929 had its first serious effects in Latvia in 1931, although, Latvia being an agricultural country, it was less violent there than in Western Europe and in the United States. Unemployment and restrictions on foreign trade followed, and were partly responsible for numerous changes of prime ministers and cabinets. The growing feeling of insecurity against aggression stimulated changes of governmental form in Poland and in the Baltic countries more or less toward some kind of restricted constitution. In Latvia, Prime Minister Karlis Ulmanis dismissed the Latvian parliament in May 1934.

The Nazis, before starting the Second World War, negotiated the Molotov-Ribbentrop understanding with the Soviets. After Poland's defeat and its fourth partition, the Finnish Winter War and the mutual assistance pacts forced by the Soviet Union on the Baltic states were the first results of the Nazi-Bolshevik understanding. The Latvian government was presented with a Soviet demand for military bases in its territory. The same thing happened to Estonia and Lithuania. Feeling trouble, the Latvian government issued extraordinary powers to its minister in London, K. Zarins, and transferred the Latvian gold fund to the United States, where it is frozen to the present time. The German occupation of Denmark, Holland, and Belgium and the Allied defeats in France prompted the Soviet Union to move faster. Pretending that the Baltic states were not capable of assuring an honest implementation of the mutual assistance pacts and were provoking border clashes, the Soviets occupied the three countries.

A Soviet puppet government was created in Latvia. It carried out parliamentary elections with only one list of candidates, and scores of the political opposition were put safely in prisons. The "newly elected" parliament proclaimed a Soviet Latvian Republic and nationalization of the banks, land, urban real estate, industry, commerce, and transport. The Soviet Latvia was "kindly admitted" by its own request to the Union of Soviet Socialist Republics. The same happened to Estonia, Lithuania, and Eastern Carelia, which was separated from Finland.

In the meantime mass arrests by the secret police started, and the Soviet penal code was introduced and applied retroactively. The members of the Latvian government, including President Ulmanis, were the first to be deported. During this first Soviet occupation,

6,041 persons received long sentences for alleged anti-Soviet activities and 1,488 persons were executed. Large-scale deportations were carried out in all the three Baltic countries on June 14, 1941. The total number deported from Latvia that day is 34,250, including 4,000 children. The deportations were carried out in a ruthless manner. People were taken by surprise in the middle of the night, families were separated, and they were allowed to take with them little more than the clothes they dressed in. Most of the Latvians were sent to an area north of the Arctic circle, thousands of them to perish in hard labor camps.[4]

Following such acts of terror by the Soviets, the German invasion on June 22, 1941 seemed like liberation, particularly when captured documents disclosed Soviet actions and future plans for mass arrests, executions, and deportations. But the harsh Nazi rule later disillusioned many people who were opposed to communism.

Documents published by the U.S. State Department reveal the goal of Nazi policy: "In the case of these areas the question arises whether they should be allotted the special task of becoming a German settlement in the future, the most suitable racial elements to be assimilated. . . . The necessary removal of considerable sections of the intelligentsia — particularly in Latvia — to the Russian nucleus area, would have to be organized." [5]

In a later stage of the war the Nazi rulers figured that an anti-Soviet Latvian Legion could be of help. Because of the Hague Convention which prohibits draft in occupied countries, the draftees were formed in a "volunteer legion," although there was practically no escape from "volunteering," and there was no use in going over to the communists, who also had draft rules of their own. While nobody believed in a German victory, a large number of Latvians felt that the Western powers would stop the communist absorption of nations at some point. An allusion to the feelings of a small nation

[4] Spekke, *op. cit.*
[5] Quoted in *ibid.*

caught against its will in the struggle of great powers is given in my stories entitled "The Dove" and "The Leavetaking."

Following the capitulation of the German armies in Kurzeme, the last stronghold in the East, where some Latvian "volunteers" fought on their side to the last, hoping for some kind of compromise that would reestablish the sovereignty of the Baltic states, the country was left to itself and to Soviet labor camps. About 6,000 escaped to Sweden in fishermen's boats, while the number of those who perished in the sea or were captured by the Russian navy is not known. About 100,000 were taken as laborers or went voluntarily to Germany.

The United States, Britain, and some other Western countries never recognized the incorporation of the Baltic states into the Soviet Union, and they are still represented in Washington and London by their ministers. But the refugees, who had to deal with reality, became emigrants and by now are scattered over the globe, mostly in the United States (about 40,000), Britain, Australia, and Canada, hoping that somehow they can help their country to be free again. This period from 1940 to the present day is reflected in many works by Latvian writers in the free world.

The end of the Second World War did not bring freedom even to Poland, whose independence was considered by the West important enough to be the final reason for war. Nevertheless the Latvian struggle for freedom is a part of a common human aspiration, a part of the faith allowed to everyone who looks upon the stars.

Knuts Lesins

TABLE OF CONTENTS

"THE LEAVETAKING," "CORDA," AND "TOYS" WERE TRANSLATED BY
HARALDS KUNDZINS, THE REST OF THE STORIES BY RUTH SPEIRS

THE WINE OF ETERNITY · SHORT STORIES FROM THE LATVIAN

THE WINE OF ETERNITY

ONCE there lived two young men. The one was a great drunkard, but the other, his friend, was poor in health and never touched a drop of wine. Both had fallen in love with the same girl. But the one who was ailing fell seriously ill, and he called for his friend when he felt his last hour drawing near.

"Listen," he said, "I have to leave this earth without having had a chance to taste its pleasures. May all its joys be yours. Only, promise me this : if you should marry Rasma, come to my grave on your wedding day and inform me of it."

The young man promised, and his friend died, as expected.

Janis Nebeda — that was his name, and it means John Have-No-Care — now proposed to Rasma. The girl said she would marry him if he promised to love her more than he loved the bottle ; she doubted whether there was room enough in one man's breast for two equally great loves. And she argued as follows :

> I would rather see a devil
> Than a man who is a drunkard ;
> When I cross myself, the devil
> Runs away — but not the drunkard.

Rasma was a beautiful girl. The young man thought and thought, and in the end he promised to give up drinking.

On his wedding day he remembered the promise he had given to

3

his friend. When the young couple were driving past the churchyard he stopped the horses, told his bride to wait for him, and went off to inform the dead man of the wedding. It is not fully known how he contrived to make his way into the underworld, but it must have been an easy matter: in those days the living and the dead kept more closely in touch than now. The dead man came to meet him, dressed in white robes; he was all smiles, congratulated him and wished him the best of luck. He himself was also doing nicely, he said. He led a carefree life, and time passed unnoticeably. Finally he offered his visitor a glass of wine. Nebeda hesitated a little, remembering his promise to Rasma, but his friend told him that this was the wine of eternity and that he would never have a chance of sampling it anywhere else. Nebeda relented. He drained the glass but was unable to detect any particular flavor, he only felt an odd kind of shiver running down his spine. He would have liked to have a good look around and see how his friend lived there, but he thought of his bride waiting in the carriage, and began to say goodbye.

"Come on, have one for the road!" his friend urged him, filling the glass once more.

"Oh well, what harm can it do me, even though it's got no taste at all," Nebeda thought, tossing it down. Slightly tipsy, he broke into a trot and ran out of the churchyard. Alas, his hurry was of no avail. Both his bride and the carriage had disappeared. But enormous trees had shot up in the place where a short while ago he had seen nothing but short grass. "It's gone to my head after all," he thought, and he shook himself and walked toward the church. When he entered he did not see any familiar faces among the congregation; he went to look for the sexton, who turned out to be a complete stranger and knew nothing about the young couple's wedding. Finally, after much searching in old church registers, he came upon the two names and an entry which said that the bridegroom had vanished in the churchyard on the day of the wedding. This had happened two hundred years ago.

4

After this revelation, Nebeda's tipsiness evaporated like the dew at sunrise. Indeed, anyone would come to his senses on such an occasion, even if he had drunk a whole barrelful of brandy and not merely two glasses of watery wine. It is rather difficult to understand, though, why people paid so little attention to a man who had drunk the wine of eternity. Perhaps it was because those who add color to their lives by taking to drink are an altogether careless lot and disinclined to do any serious investigating: they simply haven't the time, or else they want to forget such unpleasant happenings as quickly as possible. And when the new day dawns they are beset with so many cares and troubles of their own that another fellow's fate quite escapes their attention. An adroit angler can land one fish after the other from amid a school of roach without the rest realizing that their number has decreased; in the same way, a jolly crowd of men do not notice those who fall by the roadside.

As was to be expected, Nebeda made straight for the nearest inn when he had recovered from his first shock. He argued that his promise of abstinence had lost all force through the loss of his bride; furthermore, he hoped to meet some intelligent fellows who might advise him what to do next.

He was lucky, for he ran into two woodcutters who were just starting to get warm over a bottle. They emptied a few more bottles, but they were amazed when their new friend still showed no signs of intoxication. Nebeda himself was also surprised: was it possible that, after two hundred years, people had started to make such weak brandy that it had no effect upon him whatever? True, now and then there was something like a little swirl of fog in his head; it was difficult to tell whether his mood was going to be maudlin or jolly, and it was all exceedingly strange.

Then Nebeda told them his sad story. Neither of the men paid the slightest attention to it for, indeed, if one were to believe all one hears in public houses the world would look a very different place from the one we know. The one woodcutter merely inquired whether

5

Nebeda hadn't perhaps also been in the wood to listen to a certain little bird. People hereabouts, he said, were talking about a young man who had gone into the wood one morning and had heard a little bird chirping ever so prettily. When he appeared again at mid-day his hair had gone white. Now he sat in the poorhouse, and the little bird went on chirping inside his head. The other woodcutter said that eternity signified nothing if one drank for an eternity and three days: the only thing that counted were the three days. Nebeda should try this out, and he'd see how true it was. If he still wasn't drunk even then, well, it really wasn't worth while putting a glass to his lips.

As the woodcutters were pressed for time, and as their money was running out, they took their leave. But before they departed they advised Nebeda in slightly blurred accents to try the Forest Inn: there he would get drinks that would turn his very eyeballs back to front.

Nebeda reflected upon this advice and was asking the way to the Forest Inn when he was stopped by a stout man in a leather coat and Polish boots who slapped him on the shoulder and said: "I've been watching you, my lad, I see you have a strong head. That's exactly what I need. How about taking employment with me?"

Nebeda replied that his head actually felt a bit peculiar. In fact, he didn't quite know what to do with it at the moment. But if his arms were strong enough to do the work required he'd willingly serve the gentleman.

"Don't worry about that!" the fat man reassured him. "The work I offer you won't break your bones. I am Marcovius, wholesale wine merchant of Riga." And he stuck out his middle so that his coat and jacket fell open, revealing a heavy gold watch chain. "You'd have to roll out the casks and occasionally bottle the wine, and — well, I won't say anything if the wine sometimes finds its way into a fellow's throat," and he gave Nebeda a broad wink. "But, be that as it may, the accounts must not get into a muddle and your legs must not de-

6

scribe circles as you walk. Up till now I've employed highly recommended teetotallers; but all of them, the blighters, turned out to be weak in the legs and weak in the head within half a year. That's why I want to try out something different: I want to employ a powerful drunkard, a man like yourself, and let's see what happens. I've lately visited many inns to watch the drinkers, but they never walked out the same way as they had walked in. It seems that some kind providence has sent you my way. Your wages will be good. How about it? Are you willing?"

They shook hands on it, seated themselves in a fine carriage drawn by two horses, and set out for Riga. They followed the road winding along the shore of the Daugava; the sun poured the life-giving heat of summer over the countryside, and it seemed to the young man that nothing had changed: trees and grass were as verdant as ever, birds chirruped, dogs barked in doorways. But the people were different, and they were dressed differently from what he remembered.

Nebeda sat in the gently swaying carriage, thinking an inexhaustible thought, a thought for which the tardiest hours are too quick and the longest roads too short, a thought which has for generation upon generation been tinged with unstilled sadness and pain: What exactly is happening in this world, and why?

+   2   +

Nebeda had spent five years in the service of Marcovius, the wholesale wine merchant, when the latter entrusted him with the management of his cellar.

"You've mastered all the intricacies of bills and accounts, my boy, and I've always been pleased with you and your work," said Marcovius. "You've become as dear to me as if you were my own son or younger brother, and I think the time has come for you to fill a position in accordance with your abilities. There's only one thing I don't like: you never seem to be really cheerful, and perhaps you've kept too strictly to my instructions. Therefore let's both go

7

down into my cellar and enjoy the best it has to offer; for once, I want to see your cheeks glow and hear you burst into song!"

They picked up large goblets and a stout wax candle in a silver candlestick, and descended into the cellar where the huge wine vats stood side by side like menacing grey monsters confined within hoops of iron — monsters before whom a man becomes puny and insignificant, sadly conscious of his feeble powers.

But Marcovius walked past the vats, not even deigning to bestow a fleeting glance on them, and led Nebeda to the farthest end of the cellar where there were some small stone steps leading up to an iron door. When the latter was unlocked Nebeda caught sight of shelves full of large heavy bottles sitting in rows like owls in the dark.

"These are the noblest wines that ever ripened beneath the Southern sun," said Marcovius, pointing at the bottles adorned with all sorts of labels, and gazing at them as lovingly as though they were dear little children. "None but the grapevine with its delicate roots is able to draw up into itself the best living saps of the earth; apple trees, pear trees, and other fruit trees and bushes, having coarser roots, suck up the moisture of the earth indiscriminately. That is how scientists explain the wonderful qualities of the grape vine. Wine is the most felicitous dream of mysterious Nature herself. . . . And now you can choose with which to begin."

Seating himself on an empty crate, Marcovius watched the young man very curiously. Nebeda walked slowly and hesitantly along the shelves, casting uncertain glances at the rows of bottles, scanning the labels and the awe-inspiring years of vintage, unable to make up his mind which shelf to tackle first.

Marcovius burst out laughing. "Well, never mind, you're only a beginner in the fine art of wine-drinking. Allow me to do the serving this time, and I'll choose wine that does justice to a discerning palate and a strong constitution." He opened a bottle of old Burgundy. Red as rubies, clear and sparkling, it flowed into the goblets.

"It's like velvet on the tongue and like fire in the heart," said

Marcovius, rocking his head from side to side with delight. While they drank the wine they discussed Nebeda's duties as manager of the cellar and all the wonderful prospects this new job would open up to him in life. Then the old gentleman glanced at another portion of the shelves and directed Nebeda with a movement of his head to the bottle that was to be opened next. "We've lingered long enough in the kingdom of the Burgundy, this king of kings; the road ahead of us is very long, and we have to cover great distances yet. Look, this is Bordeaux, a noble wine which makes the sun shine in one's very stomach and leaves one's mouth fresh and one's head clear and light so that the most delightful thoughts can spread their wings there . . ."

The row of empty bottles along the wall became longer and longer, the candle became shorter, and Marcovius's talk grew in length and volume, but Nebeda remained as calm and quiet as ever. True, he felt the flavor of the wine caressing his palate and the aroma fondling his nostrils, but not the smallest sunbeam ever reached his head.

"Do you not like these wines, since you're not a connoisseur? Or does some sorrow weigh on your mind?" the old man suddenly asked. "Or perhaps I've been talking too much. . . . Open your heart to me, tell me whether some misfortune has befallen you. As I said before, I've become so fond of you that I'd gladly help you not only with good advice but, indeed, with everything at my disposal."

Nebeda smiled mournfully, and then he spoke as follows: "Your kindness, my master and guardian, is as great as your cellar, and your heart is of the same goodness as the wines we are drinking. It would be sinful indeed if I were to complain. Serving you, I have suffered no ill — neither in body nor in soul. I have learnt much that is good and useful to know, but there is one thing I have never been able to fathom: why does man live on this earth?"

"Ha, ha, ha . . ." the old man laughed so heartily that the gold watch chain danced a polka on his stomach. "Dear me, what a ques-

9

tion! Well, I'm blest! You don't know even the simplest thing! It is for man's pleasure and for the glory of God that man lives on this earth which is so wonderfully devised that it provides for all the spiritual and physical needs of man. You may rest assured: if man were not necessary in the scheme of things he wouldn't exist.

"But I know what is the matter with you. You are young, and young people's minds sometimes get all confused with foolish thoughts. It is not good for man to be alone. At your age, it is time to cast your eye on a different kind of beauty, one who intoxicates even more than wine and doesn't make you feel stale and sober the morning after! And Marcovius reached for a bottle of champagne; the cork flew out with explosive force, and swirling white foam like lace spurted out, followed by a stream of clear amber liquid. And when they had emptied many more bottles of this sunny foaming drink, the old man rose somewhat unsteadily to his feet and said:

"The zeal you have put into your work and into the pursuit of knowledge will open all doors to you in this old and famous town. I can vouch for that as surely as I can vouch for the purity of these French wines with which even the greatest kings have found no fault, and neither have I, and I also am a king — a king of wine! Now a new life will begin for you. The moment has come when you must seek the company of men who have risen as high as I have, and whose achievements in life are indeed noteworthy, but the main thing," and here he winked at Nebeda, as was his habit, "the main thing is that you must look for a wife. And as for your silly questions, like the one you asked me a while ago, she will drive them out of your head as easily as the champagne drives the cork out of the bottle! Then even you yourself will be amazed at your former foolishness . . ."

At this point the fumes of the wine got the better of Marcovius; the hand that held the goblet dropped wearily, and like a water plant torn loose and yielding to the current of the stream, the goblet fell to the floor, followed by the old gentleman himself who rolled heavily

10

onto the mighty row of empty bottles which jingled woefully as they felt the weight of their king upon them. Nebeda seized hold of him and laid him down on the straw mat in the corner, and Marcovius immediately sank into the sweet sleep that comes only to a man to whom all problems are clear and whose head has been deprived of all clarity by the best wines of France.

Enviously gazing at his master, Nebeda heaved a deep sigh. Then he picked up his goblet and walked along the remaining rows of bottles, opening first one and then another of those which, untasted, unenjoyed, still flanked the road the old gentleman himself had been unable to travel to the end. But neither the light wines of Alsace nor the clarets, neither the heavy golden honeyed Tokay nor the noblest wines of Italy, Spain, Greece, and Portugal had the slightest effect: his head remained perfectly clear though his heart was yearning for blissful intoxication and oblivion.

When he turned round, noticing that the burnt-down candle was on the point of going out, he saw shadows like purple-winged bats descending all about him, and a subdued humming began in all the corners, like a large orchestra of violins mournfully playing in the distance. Suddenly the candle expired, the humming of the spirits of the wine grew louder, and he could distinguish a sorrowful voice singing:

Crave for drunkenness with hopeless longing,
Never taste the joy of pleasures thronging;
No abating of your thirst and pain
Till you drink Eternal Wine again.
    Worms keep chewing, scrip, scrip, scrap,
    Good and bad are eaten up.

Joy and sorrow come in equal measure,
Anguish follows on your dance of pleasure;
Who takes more than life's allotted share
Has the burden of himself to bear.
    Worms keep chewing, scrip, scrip, scrap,
    Good and bad are eaten up.

11

Craving earthly pleasures, panting, speeding,
Feel your heart in Hell's own torments bleeding.
See the coffin waiting at your door;
Seek the road you should have sought before.
Worms keep chewing, scrip, scrip, scrap,
Good and bad are eaten up.

Terror-stricken, stumbling and crawling, Nebeda made his way to the iron door and rushed into the huge cellar, hurting himself as he knocked into the wine vats, and at last somewhat came to his senses. Everything was silent. The damp, cool air exhaled by the cellar and the vats refreshed his perspiring brow.

What a horrible song! He wondered whether he might be drunk without knowing it, and ran out of the cellar to get a lamp and find someone who would carry the old gentleman to his bed. As he ran along in the cool fresh air, the very thought of that wine cellar made him shudder.

Two young fellows came to his assistance. Seizing hold of Marcovius as though he were a barrel, they carried him upstairs into the house.

"Looks pretty well finished, he does," said one of them, heaving him into his bed.

And the fellow turned out to have been right. The next morning the old gentleman was discovered to have died without waking from his drunken stupor. The spirits of the wine had carried off his benevolent soul on their dainty little wings. And many gentlemen, who held his cellar in high esteem, said that such a death — striking at the very moment a man is intent upon his duties, as it were — was the best thing that could happen at the end of one's lifetime.

But Nebeda now became an important personage; Marcovius, who was a childless widower, had made a will in which he left Nebeda not only the wine cellar but half the rest of his property as well. The other half went to the old man's brother, Alderman Sebastian Marcovius.

12

Nebeda returned the bows of many highly respected citizens whenever he took a stroll in the streets of Riga, dressed in a black coat, a top hat on his head, and swinging a cane inlaid with silver. And many a young lady turned her smiling eyes upon him, to the annoyance and mortification of other young gentlemen who also wore black coats and top hats, and even sported canes inlaid with gold, but who had long, scraggy necks and thin legs. Nebeda went on his way, returning the smiles of all and sundry, but his heart ached: Oh, if only my father and mother could see me now, in all my glory! But his father and mother lay beneath mounds of earth, and Nebeda thought sadly of all the tender words he might have spoken to them but which had been left unsaid. And when these tender words filled his heart to overflowing, as the ice mounts the banks of a river freed from the bondage of winter, he ordered his pair of horses to be harnessed to the carriage, and set out to look for his parents' graves. But when he came to the place where he had hoped to find them he saw great numbers of neglected, overgrown mounds; the wooden crosses had long since tumbled down and rotted away, and he realized the futility of his quest. All of them were graves of the poor. He had intended to build a splendid monument for his parents, but now it was impossible, and he sank to the ground, pressing his tearstained cheek to the earth, and thinking:

> I have searched the hillside, crying,
> Left no clod of earth unlifted,
> Not a grain of sand unsifted,
> Seeking where my mother's lying.

But as he lay there, inhaling the cool fragrance of the earth and the scent of the flowers and grasses, hearing the trees swaying in the wind and the bees buzzing among the grass, a profound peace entered his heart. He felt as though something sublime and beautiful had been revealed to him, something that made eternity but a moment, and a moment — eternity. Lying there, he understood everything: grass and trees, birds, bees, and grasshoppers, all living creation which beats upon some unknown shore in a never ending, never subsiding stream of beauty, losing nothing as the sea loses nothing though its waves dash themselves against the beach.

A buzzing little insect scrambled into his ear; he woke from his reverie and, slightly dizzy, rose to his feet. He walked away briskly as though there were some urgent work waiting for him which he would enjoy doing. But soon his melancholy returned, and his steps became heavier and heavier. There stood his carriage and pair, and the few wayfarers on the road stared at it with awed admiration and respectfully raised their caps when they saw him approaching, for he was a fine gentleman. But there was not a single familiar face among them; there was no one, not even the simplest village lad, to whom he might say, slapping him on the shoulder: "Come now, don't stand on ceremony! I'm Janis Nebeda, I'm John Have-No-Care the jolly drunkard, don't you remember me?"

He caught sight of a young ploughman at work on the hillside, and he went up to him, said Good morning, and asked: "Do you know why man lives in this world?"

The ploughman stopped his horse, scratched himself behind the ear, hitched up his trousers, stared in dire perplexity at the sun, and then he said to the stranger: "Sorry, master! I quite forgot to ask my father and mother why they put a stupid fellow like me into the world. And now I haven't the time to think about such things. You've got more time than I — perhaps you could yourself . . ."

"Never mind, either you know or you don't, and there's an end to it. Here's a thaler, anyway." And Nebeda put a coin into the ploughman's hand and returned to his carriage. As he drove past the meadow he heard the ploughman singing:

> Have no time to die, must climb to
> Golden mountains that need hewing,
> Silken meadows that need mowing;
> Let those die who have the time to!

Nebeda asked himself: How long will they all live and sing like that? And he drove back to the gentlemen of Riga who had time enough to think but, instead, busied themselves with very different matters. They thirsted for power, fame, and riches; and men who had less of these things envied those who had more. It was difficult for Nebeda to enter into this spirit for he had an abundance of everything: money — and money means power — and as to fame, he was more famous than any of them. The strongest drinkers in his trade drooped like wilting flowers when they tried to match their prowess against Nebeda's; but this gave him no pleasure — indeed, what is the use of a game if one knows beforehand how it will end! He gained a considerable reputation and was always most pressingly invited to all great functions for everybody wanted to see him wield the drinking-cup: wasn't there perhaps some trick, some deception of the eye? But there was no cheating, no trick, and people shook their heads, unable to understand what was going on.

Even the Grand Duke, the Czar's cousin, happening to pass through Riga and hearing of Nebeda, expressed the wish to see him and match his strength against this great man's, for at Court he had long ceased to have any rival as far as drinking was concerned.

Six times they raised the mighty drinking horns, filled with the strongest available beer, to their lips; and then they drank brandy and other spirits until well after sunrise. Finally the Czar's cousin collapsed in his chair and left the town, humiliated and ashamed, and sent Nebeda his beaver coat as a present.

"All right, Mr. Have-No-Care, we'll see what can be done," Alderman Sebastian Marcovius said to Nebeda shortly afterwards, slapping him on the back, for it was clear that he would have to give him his beautiful daughter, Christina Maria, for a wife.

"But before we embark upon the wedding celebrations," the Alderman continued, "I'd like, for once, to see you — how shall I put it? — slightly uplifted in spirit, at least within the circle of intimate friends and members of the family. It is true, my dear departed

15

brother has always praised you most highly, but no doubt you know the saying: a lark reveals itself in song, but a man's nature in drunkenness. It is difficult for me to know what kind of person you are, for I have never seen you tipsy like other young men. There are many people who think you are proud and arrogant, and that you secretly laugh at what they say in their cups. True enough, when one has drunk a large quantity of wine one's conversation cannot exactly be likened to the Wise Sayings of Solomon, but — all of us, sometime, somewhere, are prone to weakness, we all either walk on foot or ride in carriages, and ultimately we all come to the same end. That's why such uncalled-for arrogance only annoys others and does you no good.

"Moreover, you have such an unpleasant habit of asking: Why does man live in this world? This has given offense to many because they think that in your opinion their lives are of no value whatever. And there are people in whose case such a question is apt to tear open certain wounds in their soul which haven't yet had time to heal. You will remember Councillor Knapenhauzen whose wife jumped out of the window two years ago. After this question of yours he could not sleep for three nights. At first, though you may not know it, he wanted to challenge you to a duel, but — luckily for you — he became slightly confused in the head, distributed all his property among the poor, and went into a monastery. This may be an action pleasing to God but, on the other hand, we cannot all of us be saints.

"You sometimes don't realize the dangers to which you expose yourself when you ask such a question. I have heard that you even had the audacity to put this question to the Czar's cousin. Again luckily for you, he was so excessively drunk that he forgot both question and answer, and presented you with his beaver coat. But there are occasions when the head which conceives such questions, and puts them to exalted personages, might roll off as easily as a badly sewn-on button. I'm telling you all this because I think that a frank word from your future father-in-law cannot hurt you and may, on the contrary, do us both good."

With a respectful bow, Nebeda replied: "Worthy Alderman Sebastian Marcovius, dear father of my betrothed! I have listened with the keenest interest to your instructive and well-meaning words; I shall attach great weight to your advice and shall never forget it. But may I take the liberty of remarking that your words come as a surprise to me. As you know, I have served your departed brother and my unforgettable benefactor in all humility — surely this in itself precludes any tendency towards arrogance such as is flaunted by many a high-born gentleman. And if I asked a few people the kind of question you have just referred to, it merely shows that my mind is not yet wholly enlightened. Indeed, I am very interested in the answers I receive in the course of my endeavors to find a justification for my actions, and I must admit that I have been sorely puzzled by the silence with which some people have met my question. I have come to the conclusion that this problem may not be quite so clear to everybody as it ought to be. This reflection has, in a way, rather pleased me for in this refusal to answer I seem to have found proof of my not being the only fool on this earth."

Alderman Sebastian Marcovius, slightly flushed, took hold of Nebeda by the center button of his coat, and said: "Now that you have risen so high in the world by means of your own zeal and endeavor, and assisted by unforeseen good fortune, I must confess it astonishes me greatly how you can still ask: Why does man live in this world?

"If all this is no wicked and impudent mockery on your part, I shall be so free as to express myself with some gravity. As you know, a fish enters the net with its head first and, by asking questions, many a clever man enters upon the road to Hell. God in His wisdom has concealed the ends of all things so that we, with our imperfect minds, should not start to criticize His plans. Man is part of the whole; one cannot regard him separately, lifting him out of the

17

general scheme of things. Therefore your question is the same as asking why God has created the world. Each living creature answers this question differently, each to its best ability: the bird by its song, the tree by its verdure and fruits, the foal by romping and frisking, the horse by pulling the plough without even knowing what kind of seed will fall into the furrow. But the ploughman sees to it that the furrow runs straight and that the soil is well prepared. In the same way, man answers this question by his actions, and during his lifetime he does not know what kind of seed will fall into the furrow his life has drawn. But — let this furrow, too, be straight! The Almighty has given us a mind which is but a small reflection of His own great mind, yet it is sufficient to enable man to do his work well; but it is too limited to entitle us to ask: What is the purpose and the outcome of it all?

"And now, dear sir, let us put an end to clever speeches which would in any case bore you soon enough if you indulged in carousals with other men; a mind giddy with wine sometimes recognizes even the value of stupidity which brings people closer together than too great cleverness — he, he, he! . . . Therefore, when we meet again be sure to have drunk something strong so that we may sit together as equals!"

+   4   +

Nebeda bought a diamond ring and a necklace of the most precious pearls of the East for Christina Maria. When he went home and examined his purchases he was plunged into profound grief. Oh, if only he could have given Rasma such magnificent jewelry! And many other things as well — silks and velvets, and ermine wraps. But now she was gone, and she had never known his embrace, never felt the caressing touch of luxurious fabrics on her skin . . .

He called at the house of Alderman Sebastian Marcovius and fastened the pearl necklace around Christina Maria's neck which was as white and pure as the gentle moonlight at the time of the alder

18

blossom, and he put the ring on her finger which was so fragile that it seemed a mouse could easily bite it in two. These little fingers of hers, deftly fluttering like white doves, busied themselves with silken threads at dainty embroidery: the sun itself smiled there, roses and lilies blossomed in profusion, and deer trod the green turf. Thus, on cushion covers and tablecloths, her dreams burgeoned forth and mirrored the world as poets and children see it on days of happiness — and, indeed, that is why poets and children are so dear to a woman's heart. Placed between the two, as it were, she works her own kind of poetry with patient thrusts of the needle, combining usefulness and beauty.

For a while Christina Maria admired herself and her new jewelry in the mirror, but then her mood changed, and she was gently vexed — like a butterfly accidentally wafted into the room by the breezes of springtime and lost among the Alderman's heavy dark oak furniture, bronze-studded chests, and candlesticks. She kissed Nebeda right on the mouth and, thereafter, he dared not open it again but sat, silent and thoughtful, in the big chair.

Christina Maria seated herself on the arm of his chair, put her little hand behind the back of his neck in such a way that she could admire the sparkling diamond on her finger, and said with a sigh: "Your presents are costly and beautiful, dear Johannes, and you know that a woman's foolish mind is easily captivated by such things, no matter how modest and undemanding she pretends to be, but a smile lighting up the loved one's face is an even more beautiful present. Alas, my heart is sometimes heavy with misgivings . . . Why is your brow clouded, why are your lips cool and your hands so hard? And your glance never rests on anything, it strays in all directions as though you were trying to catch sight of something no one else can see. Believe me, I'd wear these jewels much more gladly if I could share the invisible burden which seems to weigh so heavily on your mind.

"My precious, my dearly beloved Christina Maria," Nebeda re-

19

plied, pulling himself together and timidly stroking the finger on which she wore the ring, "my hands are hard because they aren't yet accustomed to touching such dainty limbs as yours; my lips are cool because they've had little occasion to say warm, loving words; and my brow is clouded because there is a certain worry that greatly depresses me. Your father is displeased with me because my head is too steady and won't droop at carousals like the heads of other men who remember neither the drinks nor the conversation they've had in the course of the evening. And there will no wedding unless I appear before your father in a state of intoxication. That is what worries me . . ."

"What nonsense!" cried Christina Maria. "As though it were he, and not I, who is going to be married! I shouldn't in the least want you to be intoxicated with anything but . . ." here she broke off, and blushed. "My father has probably been incited against you by that old Junker, Krummenbach, who is a great drunkard and would dearly like me to marry his son. But the son is just as bad as the father, and his laugh is about as much as I can bear. It sounds as if it came out of an empty tin can — which serves him as a head, I suppose, for I've seldom heard him pronounce more than three sentences altogether. They are always the same, and he has learnt them by heart — one from his grandmother, and it is 'oho,' the other from his father, and it sounds like 'aha,' and the third sentence, the longest of them all, comes from his mother and consists of 'how nice!' The Krummenbachs, both father and son, hate you and try to blacken you as much as they possibly can. For instance, I've heard them say that it wasn't quite clear how exactly my dear uncle met his death that night, and they've even suggested that you might be in some way connected with the King of Darkness . . .

"Of course, there's nothing but envy behind it all. Forgive me for repeating such rubbish, but their intrigues make me furious!"

Slightly flushed with rage, her eyes flashing — and this made her still more beautiful — she jumped off the chair and brandished her

20

little fists. But she happened to catch sight of herself in the mirror, and her anger passed. With the slyest and most ravishing smile ever seen on a girl's face, she turned to Nebeda and said: "Am I to teach you what to do?! Really, there are times when one despairs of the so-called cleverness of men, but — that's why we women are here in the world: to smooth out such lapses in your intelligence. Can't you pretend a little? Surely you could at least fall asleep at the table if they are so anxious that you should do it! It can't be so very difficult, can it, considering that you've seen so many others doing it . . ."

Nebeda frowned. "Indeed, that wouldn't be difficult, dear Christina Maria. But, all the same, I am afraid they wouldn't quite believe me . . . And if they did they might like it so much that I'd have to do it often in order not to arouse suspicion. But the point is that I'd really like to drink something at last that would lighten my mind and free it from the fetters of reality . . ." He jumped to his feet and paced up and down in great agitation. "Oh, how I wish I could be like other men, even a fool like that Junker, young Krummenbach!"

Christina Maria smiled: "Thank goodness, you can never become like him! But if you have set your heart on getting drunk like other men . . . well, I know where I can go to ask for advice about your problems. There is an old woman — many things are known to her . . . Be patient, wait for a few days, and then I'll tell you what is to be done or where you can find a wine that will go straight to your head."

"If such a wine could be found I'd spare neither money nor words of gratitude," Nebeda exclaimed. "It would practically mean the salvation of my unhappy soul . . . But I fear that such hopes will prove as vain as all my other hopes have been."

"Have faith, dearest, have faith!" And after another kiss from her, this time on his brow, Nebeda left the house of Alderman Sebastian Marcovius.

21

In olden times people lived more leisurely. Solid, low-walled inns stood at all the crossroads. There, before continuing on their way, travelers could reconsider their various business matters; and, upon mature reflection, quite a few of these matters lost their urgency and others turned out to be altogether dispensable. Many such shelved transactions piled up at the Forest Inn. Gradually, time did away with them and the travelers alike, and finally did away even with the Forest Inn itself. It was turned into a smithy. And where the merry crowd of unhurried travelers had clinked their drinking cups there was now a loud hammering as modern fleet-footed horses were being shod. In the First World War the smithy was hit by some grenades. Years went by, and then the remains of the walls were used for building a smaller house in which a petrol station was installed. The roads became smoother, people traveled faster and faster — but did it make them any better or happier? They merely carried their sorrows more swiftly over all the many roads. No longer was there the Forest Inn where they could leave their worries behind, nor was there the benevolent innkeeper, Giksts, who knew the remedies for every kind of heartache.

People said that his mother had been a witch. Maybe it was from her he had inherited his knowledge of diverse roots and herbs which he brewed and mingled with the drinks he served, refreshing parched throats and mitigating all kinds of sorrows. His cellar was always full of mysterious jars and bottles, and each had its own special healing-power. People merely had to whisper into Giksts' ear what was the matter with them, and straight away he went to look for the appropriate bottle. If the ailment was rather unusual the search for a suitable remedy took longer, but in the end everybody got what he desired.

There was a potion for unhappy love; it had a bitter-sweet taste like alder berries, and it immediately cured a lad's gloom so that hopeful lilacs seemed to blossom forth in his head even in the se-

22

verest frost. Another potion was for men with quarrelsome wives; it was heavy and sweet as honey, and it had a prolonged effect on the brain, making the drinker mild and lenient. There was a potion to be taken if a man suffered from a ferocious mother-in-law; it was black because the roots of a certain shrub had soaked in it for a very long time, and it filled one's ears with a delightfully gentle sound like the wind sighing among the trees of a forest, so that the mother-in-law's words were swallowed up in it as if they were strummings of a grasshopper. And there was a potion named "Devil's Growl," a potent brew indeed; the very first sip made one roll one's eyes and, for a while, feel very brave — which was useful for courting a girl, giving one's rival a thrashing, or speaking up for oneself in a court of law. There were potions as red as the berries of the mountain ash, and these were for old men. They made the drinker forget the things he had not accomplished and remember everything pleasant that had happened to him in the course of his life; in his thoughts he would stroll, clad in white raiment, through the garden of his past which spread about him free of weeds. And Giksts the innkeeper had many other potions besides, strong and beneficent, which swept all afflictions away as a river the leaves of autumn and the blossoms of spring.

Nowhere else was there such thinking of tremendous thoughts as at the Forest Inn. There seemed to be enough of them to turn the world upside down but, alas, the thoughts were as unsteady as the drinkers' legs. Many a man only noticed that the leaves were budding on the trees, or the trees shedding their leaves, when he made his way home at nights and gazed into the sparkling stars. Others were hardly aware of the changing seasons as they sat in the inn, rarely looking out of its small windows. Many a granary stocked with rye and wheat was transformed into a stream of gold which rapidly flowed to the inn and evaporated in the form of strange dreams in drunken men's heads.

Giksts usually did not drink with his customers; but there were times when he was seized by some fierce whirlwind, as it were, and then he became his own best customer. Whoever happened to call on such an occasion was feasted and given drinks without having to spend a farthing.

One such evening, when merriment crackled in the air like fire among dry straw, and when lame Karlis scraped tunes on his fiddle like the chirpings of drunken crickets, a carriage stopped outside the inn. A pale gentleman, a black cloak flung across his shoulders, asked for a night's lodging. He was shown to a small chamber which happened to be vacant; barely looking at it, he declared himself satisfied. He appeared to be neither young nor old, and his face seemed little used to smiling.

"And what might be the gentleman's name?" asked Giksts who had consumed a large quantity of "Bachelors' Tears" and was itching for a chat with the stranger. "And which road might he be taking?"

"There was a time when my name was Have-No-Care, but it has changed to Full-Of-Care, if you really wish to know, though I can't see what you gain by it. As to which road I'll be taking — how can one ever be sure of roads? There are some that begin at the point where one thought they ended, and there are others which end the moment the horses are harnessed . . ."

"Yes, happiness sometimes changes into misery faster than the sun goes down in the sky, and the reverse is just as true. But in such a case a taste of my assortment of drinks wouldn't come amiss to the gentleman. Come, let us drink — today I'm the one who pays!"

The visitor seemed to give a start, and he smiled for the first time. "I have already heard about your drinks, Giksts. They are praised by all whose throats are like bottomless pits. I'd very much like to see how much truth there is in what people say."

"You've come to the right place, sir! No one has ever left my inn the same as he entered." And Giksts led his guest into the main room where the fiddle was playing amid a babel of voices and some of the revellers were stamping their heavy feet to the rhythm of the

24

music. "What drinks does your heart desire? Which one does your throat thirst after? What cares are weighing you down? Tell me, and I'll put the right remedy on the table."

"I am beset by many cares," the visitor answered evasively. "But there is one of my cares which is worse than the others, and if you can guess it I'll pay you three days' bills and add a cap full of gold."

Both stepped forward to the center of the room where the stranger stopped for a moment, dazed with the light and the smoke; then, followed by inquisitive glances, he sat down at the large table laden with food and drink. Giksts quickly ran down to the cellar and returned with some dusty bottles which he put on the table, saying: "Our new guest is suffering from certain misfortunes, but he refuses to disclose them, and therefore I've tried to guess them to the best of my ability and understanding. Come, taste some of these drinks, and see if you don't get as tipsy as the others!"

Eager hands hastened to fill the newcomer's glass. He emptied it again and again, sampling the drinks, but his expression did not change although the merriment around him ran higher and higher.

"Are my drinks not to the gentleman's liking?" asked Giksts, regarding him with close attention.

"Your drinks are good, they are sweet, they are strong, but they are not what my soul desires . . . They are like a juniper branch: it catches fire and emits white smoke, but does not burn away; it still remains — a blackened branch with scorched needles . . . the same old cares," the visitor replied pensively.

The revellers exchanged glances, and became quieter. Several of them drew closer to the stranger and began to talk to him. "Are there really such cares that can't be put to flight with a song and a good quantity of drink?" asked lame Karlis who had stopped playing and came to join the others, anxious not to miss the food and drink the innkeeper was so lavishly providing.

"There are no greater sufferings than those that are caused by

25

love," declared a young man. "Ever since my girl died I've felt as if I were only a shadow of myself."

"Love causes great sufferings," the stranger agreed. "But is it possible to love what no longer exists? You loved your own hopes and joys. You mourn for the broken mirror which no longer reflects your smile. And now you love the memory of your hopes and joys. He who lives in memories thinks a great deal. And he who thinks cannot be happy. You must not think!"

"The greatest sufferings of all are caused by a bad conscience," remarked another man.

"Yes, those are also great sufferings," the stranger said. "A broken word is like a thorn in the seat of one's trousers — one cannot sit down anywhere in peace. And the ill done to another can only be forgiven by him, never by oneself. But a bad conscience makes the heart grow wiser."

"Are there still greater sufferings in the world, since ours seem so insignificant to you?" asked a third.

"Your sufferings are like your drunkenness — they all evaporate . . . But one is tormented by the greatest sufferings of all when one cannot understand the joys of others, when one has missed one's time and everything has lost its meaning. Our hearts cannot be filled with joys of the past. Each period of time has its own attitude to life, its own joys and sorrows. Where is your victory when your enemies have long been dead, and when those who loved you are no longer there to witness it? . . . No, there is no drink here from which one wouldn't sober down when one lies in the coffin, there is none here that would make one forget there is a tomorrow!"

"Upon my word, sir," cried Giksts, "you're not talking nonsense, and your speech is that of an educated man, but such talk would be more suitable in a graveyard than at my inn!"

"Look," the stranger exclaimed scornfully, "isn't this a graveyard? Isn't each of you a monument to someone dead, to father or mother? Isn't each of you a gravestone at the head of a dead and buried hope? Time hasn't yet revealed this to you. But time is neither short nor long, it passes, and it stands still. He who looks beyond it will realize that there is nothing here but graves."

Giksts inclined his head and carefully studied the speaker. "Yours is a strange kind of intoxication, sir . . . But one should rejoice over a bottle while it lasts, without thinking that in the end it will be empty. Otherwise, what's the use of putting it on the table — and it's the same with people's lives."

The stranger smiled sadly; the revellers had gradually fallen silent while listening to the conversation between him and Giksts, and seizing his opportunity, he began to sing a melancholy song:

> Crave for drunkenness with hopeless longing,
> Never taste the joy of pleasures thronging;
> No abating of your thirst and pain
> Till you drink Eternal Wine again.
> Worms keep chewing, scrip, scrip, scrap,
> Good and bad are eaten up.

"It's really too bad that a learned gentleman should suffer from such deep grief," lame Karlis interrupted him. "Look at me, I can enjoy myself only on one leg, but with a good laugh I can frighten the Devil himself away!" And he started to play the naughtiest and merriest ditty ever composed:

> In the coffin, where I shall lie soon,
> pidiralla, pidiralla,
> I'll spit at the ceiling and whistle a tune,
> pidiridirallala.

In the meantime Giksts had quietly put a large jug on the table, and now he nodded to the stranger. With an indifferent and doubtful air, the latter filled his glass from it and slowly began to drink. A change came over his face, and surprise gradually dawned upon it like a large exclamation mark. When the others saw this they eagerly filled their glasses from the same jug, but their faces grew long and they fell silent.

27

"Listen, Giksts," shouted the stranger, "that's the right one, yes, it's the same one! It's as refreshing as the water from the spring which I drank as a boy!" He raised the jug to his mouth and drained it dry as though overcome by terrible thirst. And he became merrier and merrier, stepped into the middle of the room, slapped lame Karlis on the shoulder, and began to skip and jump with the rhythm of the music, joining in the song:

> Grudging curmudgeons are digging my grave,
> pidiralla, pidiralla,
> But I'm not afraid of the grave, I am brave,
> pidiridirallala.

And while he was thus spinning about to the wild music those nearest to him noticed that he was becoming more and more transparent; the light of the big lamp shone right through him, and his body no longer cast a shadow.

"Hah," he shouted at the top of his voice, "now I recognize you, my own family's great-grandchildren! Giksts, you're of my father's brother's stock!" He opened his arms to embrace Giksts; and then they all saw his face gradually disappear from view like a red-hot sieve cooling down and losing its glow, and the only thing still visible was a big shiny nose which bore a striking resemblance to the innkeeper's.

"Go and rest in peace, Janis! Now I know who you are . . ." Giksts said in a low voice, so terrified that he could scarcely speak. "It was for your sins that I had to become an innkeeper . . ." And the guest disintegrated like a column of smoke in a low wind. All that remained was a little heap of dust on the floor.

At the sight of these uncanny happenings the revellers, who had first stood dazed and motionless with wonder, almost jumped out of their skins with fright. Helter-skelter, forgetting bottles, glasses, food and caps, screaming, pushing, getting stuck in the doorway, hurling abuse at each other, they rushed out of the inn. The last one to escape was lame Karlis who had abandoned the fiddle but held

28

the bow in a tight grip as if it were a rescuer's hand stretched out to him from goodness knows where.

In the general confusion somebody must have knocked the big lamp off the table, for the Forest Inn went up in flames. Old people who still remembered that event said that the inn burnt like the Devil's torch, hurling blue, green, and red flashes of light and white sheaves of fire into the darkness of the night; then there was a big explosion, probably caused when the fire reached Giksts' store of powerful drinks. Nobody knew what had happened to Giksts himself. Some years later, workmen from the neighboring district (the local inhabitants would not go near the place for anything in the world) started to clear away the rubble, and they discovered a skeleton with a bottle in his hand. They concluded that it must be Giksts.

The jug which the innkeeper had placed before his relative had contained nothing but pure water. This was disclosed by the serving girl who had managed to escape with the others from the Forest Inn that night. Giksts had angrily said to her: "I seem to have a very odd customer tonight. If only he isn't in some way related to the spirits of the dead! He doesn't get drunk, no matter what one puts before him. It's ridiculous to waste good stuff on a man like that. Go, my girl, fetch me a jug of water, and let's see what he says!" She went out and filled the jug from the little stream which ran past the old churchyard where Nebeda had paid a visit to his friend two hundred years ago. And thus, perhaps, he had stepped back into the natural conditions of his existence, in accordance with which he ought to have died long, long ago.

But knowledgeable folk later arrived at the conclusion that it had probably never crossed such a drunkard's mind to drink plain water. Therefore he had knocked about in the world, not knowing what was good for him. Indeed, what is water if not the wine of eternity which washes away blossoms and decay alike, makes the rain fall and the trees grow verdant, and flows, a mighty stream, through the earth's foundations — past and beyond men's insignificant lives.

29

THE TAILOR AND THE WOLVES

AND this horn, which is called a French horn, you shall keep hanging in a place of honor in this farmhouse, from generation to generation, from son to son, and you shall keep it clean and well polished so that it always stays bright and gathers neither dust nor cobwebs. I do not mind, on the contrary, I gladly give my consent if, on a great occasion, someone who knows how to do it — particularly if he is a member of the Sleinis family — plays a tune on it which is pleasing to God. But children must not meddle with it, and it must not be lent to anybody who is only a beginner in the beautiful art of music and does not know himself what will come out at one end of the horn when he blows down the other. May this horn always remind you how kindly God in His wisdom can look upon man, and how great is the power of musical tunes. For, if it were not as I say, there would be neither I myself nor my descendants. How it all came to pass, and how this horn once saved me from deadly peril, shall be recounted forthwith.

This is an extract from the last will and testament of Great-Grandfather Gusts Sleinis; it is remembered by his family in connection with an event which took place about the middle of the last century, and of which only the bare facts are set down in the testament. But the story, though no longer preserved in the old-fashioned language

30

of his day, has survived in great detail in the minds of the older generation who had heard it from Great-Grandfather's own lips.

+ + +

Darta Skara, who was a relative on my mother's side, was to be married at Christmas. We were to play at her wedding — I, Duka the tailor, and Andrejs, the sexton's son. I was eighteen years old at the time. I had always been a great lad for learning things by heart and, in a manner of speaking, the sexton was going to give me some instruction though he mostly made me help Andrejs look after the vestry, light the candles, and work the organ bellows. Those mighty pipes of the Lord God had a strange effect on me, and I'd have preferred to stand about and listen, sunk into thought, but it always happened that I had to get busy on the bellows when the organ was played. The sexton noticed that I liked music; he himself could play several instruments, and he taught me the French horn. Soon after, we became friends with Duka the tailor who had recently come to our district and who played the fiddle. The sexton's lad, Andrejs, played the big trombone, and the three of us together could make quite a noise. And if somebody joined us with another fiddle or with a clarinet, well, then we were a real band. Now and then the farmers invited us to play at weddings and on other important occasions, and we were well fed and feasted for our trouble.

We were at church that evening, and it was arranged that we would drive to the wedding together with the guests. But Duka had left his fiddle at home; he lived down here in the village, and he thought he would fetch it on our way past. Peteris Skara, the young wife's cousin who was to take us along in his sledge, had meanwhile disappeared; very likely he wanted to talk to Liza and ask her to come along too, for he had his eye on her, but she was one who needed a powerful lot of persuading. Duka lost his patience and went off to fetch his fiddle; he hadn't yet come back when Peteris arrived. Peteris had managed to get Liza into his sledge and was

31

ready to drive off. It would have been quite easy for him to take me in his sledge and drive past the tailor's house and pick him up, too; but Peteris only thought of his own interests and was scared that Liza might change her mind. He shouted to me that farmer Raugs had room in his sledge, and drove off like the wind. Unfortunately it turned out that Raugs had already left with Andrejs. And so there was nothing but confusion, all because of this girl Liza and the tailor's fiddle. When Duka came we both stood in the empty church square by the posts to which the horses had been tethered, and the blizzard which had begun at lunchtime sent big wet snowflakes spinning all around us.

When I had told the tailor everything about how it had happened that we were left behind to make our way on foot, he began to swear at me. This did not improve matters at all. When he had relieved his feelings his voice was no longer quite so loud, and he said some words in Russian which probably weren't very polite. Together with Vilums Preiss, he had taken part in the peasant revolt at New Bebri in his young days. For this he had been punished and had to run the gauntlet and was deported to Siberia; but later he was pardoned, and came home. His legs were a bit stiff because of all the beatings he had got, and he had developed quite a gift for swearing while he was in Siberia. For a while he figured he'd ignore the whole business of the wedding, and go home. His rage had so frightened me that I made no attempt to argue with him. I must say I, myself, was angry enough about Peteris Skara's perfidy. But with the tailor it was like this: if one agreed with him, or at least didn't contradict him, he calmed down; then he would growl, and growl some more, and change his mind right around in the opposite direction. The same thing happened now: I don't know why it struck him that I'd be simply delighted if he went home and there was no music at the wedding.

"You can't fool me, my boy, I know what you're thinking! Don't imagine you'll run home!" he said firmly. "I don't care if my legs

32

crumble away beneath me, but when I made the bridegroom's clothes I promised to play at his wedding, and play I will. Come on!"

True enough, it wasn't really such a problem to walk there — five miles to go — and for me it was nothing at all, but the tailor didn't get on so well because of his stiff legs and the snowdrifts on the road; what with all the swearing and panting, we barely covered half the way in an hour. But now the blizzard had died down, the wind was no longer against us, and the tailor was in a better mood. He reckoned that we'd get there just in time and that we had the right to demand an extra large glass of vodka. He got busy sorting out all the words he was going to use when he swore at Peteris; he intended to use them in such a way that the young couple and all the wedding guests would get their share too — then his wounded self-esteem would be completely gratified. Next, he discussed all the good things we were going to eat at the wedding; he spoke with such relish that my mouth began to water and we stepped along more briskly.

The moon rose behind clouds cut to ribbons by the wind. I don't know why, but all this brightness suddenly made me feel lonely and sad, as if something had pierced me right through. Perhaps it was the after-effect of the tailor's powerful swearing which had been quite unjust, and to which I had made no answer. For a while I sank into my private sorrow and dreamed how much better it would be to sit in a warm room at home instead of trudging all these miles, despised and abused, with that fool of a tailor. I woke from my thoughts at the sound of a long-drawn howling which came from somewhere near the wood. The tailor stopped.

"Did you hear that?"

"Yes, what is it? Dogs?" I asked, but I knew quite well what it was although I had never heard anything like it.

"These, my lad, are the songs of uninvited wedding guests," the tailor said grimly and increased his speed. To tell the truth, a shiver went down my spine; but close at hand, to the right, there were some houses, and we could see lighted windows. Dogs began to bark ahead of us, and I felt more safe. I had heard people talk about wolves, but nobody had ever seen them on the road near the village. Soon the howling stopped, and we continued on our way. The tailor kept silent. The snow crunched under our feet, and there was no other sound on the whole wide snow-covered plain.

Somebody had driven along here: there were fresh tracks in the road, and they somehow gave me courage. We passed houses and a grove of birch trees, and came to the pastures with their small bushes, and saw the edge of the wood in the distance. There were still a couple of miles to go till we reached the Skara farmstead. Suddenly there was that terrible howling again, and this time it sounded much closer.

The tailor turned round and looked at me. I tried not to show what a fright I had got, but Duka seemed to be under the impression that I was scared.

"Well, what do you think? Do you want to take to your heels and run home?" he asked.

"I don't know, master, but perhaps, to be on the safe side, we might turn in at the Klimza farm. Couldn't we persuade them to drive us to the wedding? After all, it isn't very far, is it?"

The tailor also seemed to have misgivings, but once again his devilish obstinacy got the better of him, and we didn't turn back. To give him his due, he wasn't a man to be easily frightened, and he grew even bolder when he noticed that someone else was afraid.

"Let's go on, lad! I've heard this music before . . ." Here he broke off.

We had caught sight of them. The wolves were near the edge of the wood where the moon shed its brightest light over the white plain. There were about five of them. They had run out into the open and were sniffing and sporting as if playing a game in the moonlight. One of them raised his head.

"The devils, they've spotted us!" said the tailor, and his voice

34

seemed rather hoarse to me. I was overcome with panic, I'd have turned and fled as fast as my legs could carry me.

"Are you crazy, son?" and the tailor got hold of me by the shoulder. "How can you get away, look!"

The pack of wolves were making for us, smoothly running in a straight line, one at the head, the others following. "At such times, Gusts, forward, nothing but forward, come what may; if you're lucky — well and good, keep at it; if not — it's the will of God!" And the tailor suddenly stepped out smartly, quite forgetting his stiff legs. I thought he had gone out of his head — he ran straight at the wolves! But, as it turned out, there was sense in his running. I understood quickly enough what it was all about when he left the road and, huffing and panting, began to scramble up a hillock which was overgrown with junipers and had a tall birch tree in the middle.

"But, master, do you think we'll manage to get up that birch tree?" I asked.

"Who wants to get up there, you fool! A hill is always a good thing. A beast is just like a man: he loses confidence when he has to storm a bastion. It always rouses the courage of the defenders, and it makes the attacker more respectful. Have you got a strong knife on you?"

"I've got a knife, yes," I said, "but there's a whole pack of those devils!"

"They're not the only kind I've seen," roared the tailor. Some defiant madness seemed to have broken loose in him; and later, when I reflected on it all, I remembered that this man had been a rebel and that he had run the gauntlet of a thousand soldiers. Perhaps, compared to that, four or five wolves were nothing to him.

Now we had climbed to the top of the knoll. There was a large clear space round the birch tree. The wolves were aiming to get at us, there was no doubt about it. They had formed into a drawn-out single file, and they came running towards our hillock, their noses to the ground.

35

Duka, for reasons I don't know, spoke in a half-whisper; but his words came very fast and with such authority as if he were the commander of a regiment. "A wolf isn't like a dog, he doesn't go for your legs, he tries to get straight at your throat and to pull you down. And when he jumps at you he'll always jump slightly sideways. It's important to know that — only, don't let him pull you down when he jumps, stick your knife between his ribs. But wait . . . we'll first try to calm them down."

The tailor took his fiddle and bow out of their case and put them down beneath the birch tree; then, in a threatening manner, he made off towards the wolves with the case in his hands. Well, that really was the last straw!

"What are you up to, with that box?" I shouted after him.

"You'll see! Oh, the devil take it, I'm quite muddled — pull out your horn! Blow it as hard as you can when I tell you!"

I had scarcely opened my knife and got my horn ready when Duka made a dash to the edge of the slope and threw the violin case at the wolves. There was a mighty howling and barking, and I couldn't for the life of me understand what was going on. I had raised the horn, ready to blow, but I must admit that in my excitement my lips and fingers didn't obey me — there was only a burbling squeak, when the tailor shouted: "Wait, there's no sense in doing it now!"

There was a great commotion going on around the box. I could not believe that the wolves would eat a violin case, and as a matter of fact they didn't. But, as they pounced upon it, one of them probably got bitten, and the others, smelling blood, had set upon him. The snow was swirling; the big milling knot of brutes howled and snarled, and in a few minutes there were only four wolves left. There were dark patches of blood in the snow. I was quite numb with terror and amazement when I saw that sight.

"God Himself has lent us a hand," declared the tailor. "Now they won't be so hungry. Come on, quick, to the birch tree! And get busy on your horn!"

36

We settled down in the middle of the clearing, and I had just raised the horn to my lips when some of the grey-coats came flying up the hill. But it was quite true: they were no longer so fierce. They stopped, and they stood among the junipers, their eyes shining with a bluish-green light — like stars in a big frost. One of them, probably their leader, came out into the open, sniffed at our tracks, and stood facing the birch tree. I got my breath back and blew the French horn with all my might. I don't know what kind of tune it was, and very likely it wasn't a tune at all; I had never heard myself produce such disconnected sounds before. But the effect was quite tremendous, the grey-coats jumped with fright, the whole pack ran off and huddled together at the side of the hillock.

"Take it easy," the tailor said in my ear, "give us a nice mellow note!"

All his fear seemed to have gone, or maybe he had never been afraid at all; he set about things more boldly than he would have among hives full of bees.

"Let's see what my little beauty can do!" He smiled, picked up his fiddle and strummed away like a madman and made straight for the biggest wolf.

"Devil's brats," he yelled, "have you ever heard the Musicians of the Lord God?"

Then something happened that quite took my breath away. When Duka came closer the wolf scuttled off and ran behind the juniper bush, and there he sat down, raised his head to the sky, and set up a long, long dismal howl. After a while another wolf joined in.

"You see, even a wolf has a feeling for music in his soul," the tailor boasted, "when you blew your horn they scampered away, but now they're just like friends!"

In my amazement I had stopped blowing my horn and, quite frankly, things were altogether beyond me. But Duka kept walking round and round the juniper bush and playing his fiddle, at first some lively airs — polkas and waltzes — and then he passed on to very mournful tunes, and all the time he walked about among the wolves as if they were dogs. There seemed to be some kind of supernatural power in the tailor; I knew we were safe as long as he kept up his playing, and I became quite calm. Then Duka, still playing, stepped a little closer to me and said: "Don't stand about doing nothing! Cut up some junipers while I'm giving them a concert; we'll try to light a fire."

I fastened the horn to my arm and started to chop away at the junipers which grew on the farther side of the birch tree. Meanwhile the master tailor went on playing, and the wolves, huddled together in a little flock, stretched their necks and raised their heads to the moon, and now and then they howled; it was quite weird to see and hear it all.

When I had cut down a lot of juniper branches and torn some bark off the birch tree, I tried to light a fire. The junipers burst into bright crackling flames and the wolves stopped their howling and made off; for a while we thought they had run away for good. But that was too much to hope for. When the master tailor stopped playing and came to the fire, rubbing his hands, they appeared again.

"They must have taken a fancy to my playing!" Duka said. "You'll have to get busy on your horn again, Gusts. It isn't likely that we'll get a good fire going."

He was right; the juniper needles smoked but the green branches did not kindle so easily and, however hard I tried, the fire was on the point of going out.

"There's nothing for it, we'll have to effect a break-through," the master tailor announced energetically. "Come on, let's spit in our hands, Gusts my boy, and play away at the hymn 'The Lord God is our strong support,' and then — with the help of God — we'll get through to the road. I don't think they'll attack us now. Still, we'd better play while we're walking; we won't keep them cheerful much longer if we hang about here."

We stood up side by side, Duka and I, and began to play the

38

hymn. Never have I blown a French horn with such devotion as that night on the hillock, facing a pack of wolves in the moonlight. Now and then my eyes filled with tears. Was it really my fate to die such a dreadful death? Or would our music save us? We had done no harm, we were only poor musicians who had to play at a wedding. The bright sky with its many sparkling stars spread above us, and the whole of God's beautiful world seemed to assure me that we would be saved. I very much didn't want to die just when I was reflecting upon things that had never crossed my mind in my first fright.

We had reached the third verse of the hymn when the wolves suddenly stirred. But they weren't trying to get at us; they scampered down the hillock. And when we stopped playing we heard the sound of sleighbells coming from the road ahead of us.

"Heaven forbid," cried the master tailor, "what if someone comes to grief now that we're safe! They probably won't attack a sledge on the open road — but let's hurry, our music may still be useful!"

But there was no longer anything to fear; when the sledge came into view on the road the wolves trotted off and rounded the corner of the wood from where they had come. The horse between the shafts was almost out of control; it flew along the road through the snowdrifts, mightily kicking up its legs as if ridden by the Evil One himself, and scattering silvery clouds in all directions.

"Come on, my lad, blow your horn — for the horse, this time," said the master tailor. "You should know by now what kind of tune appeals to each creature!"

But it was enough that we ran along the road to meet the sledge. The driver managed to get control over the horse.

It was Peteris, with the young husband.

"Well, you scoundrels, now you know what wolves are, eh? There you were, two men, bolting like rabbits with sledge and all, but we've been playing them all the wedding tunes!" shouted the tailor at the top of his voice.

"I'm sorry, master! Don't bear us a grudge," said the young husband. "When we noticed that you weren't there, and when no sense could be got out of this blockhead Peteris, we set out at once to meet you. We heard that hymn, and we couldn't understand what had come over you and why you were playing by the roadside, but when we saw the wolves running down the hill—God have mercy!—I cursed and cursed myself; it was all my fault, I should have seen to it that you were conducted to the wedding with full honors. But step in, both of you. Sit down, and here's a drop of something; it's good for fright, and it will save you from dying of cold!"

Duka took a powerful pull at the bottle; the liquor gurgled down his throat, and his mood improved at once. "Well, farmer, you know best; never mind, why shouldn't I play to wolves . . . But look here — if Gusts hadn't been there with his mighty horn you'd be looking for our bones now!"

It was only then that I realized what a tremendous fellow this Duka was, and in my heart I forgave him all the bad language he had heaped upon me. After all, it cannot be denied: if it hadn't been for his advice I'd have been eaten up long ago together with my horn.

We sat down in the sledge and drove to the Skara farm. There was feasting and music till sunrise, and then for another two days, and we were right in the thick of it all the time. Then we were driven home like the Kings of Poland themselves, with shouts of "hurrah" and with presents and silver money. Only Duka the master tailor was sad. "Look," he said, "feasts pass just the same as dangers, and never again will there be such a wedding, and never again will there be wolves who listen to my music!"

 **A STRING OF BEADS**

ANSIS, the twenty-year-old farmhand, walked about sunk into deep, gloomy thought. He had never been talkative, but now he seemed struck altogether dumb. He had no luck in love. Anna, with her wiles, her supple young body, and her firm full breasts, had completely turned his head.

In the spring, when he came to the farm, it had amused Anna to tempt the strong, shy lad with the blue eyes of a child, and to throw him into confusion. A smile here and there, sly questions and, as though accidental, a touch of her soft hand and her body brushing against him, rich with the promise of physical passion — it was enough to make his young heart throb with love.

But when he had at last summoned all his courage and tried to draw her into a close embrace, he was foiled.

"You're too young and green, my boy, and you're neither the first nor the last to be after me," she said, sliding out of his arms.

This had happened on a Sunday, when he was dressed up in a clean shirt and his best suit and had even put oil on his fair hair which usually resembled an unruly bundle of straw. He was not quick-witted, and he could think of no retort; he merely blushed and slunk away to the back of the garden. There, by the old bathhouse, he silently pondered over the injustice done him.

41

In the evening he went to the farmers' dance and, skulking in corners, watched Anna dance with others. He was so strong that he could have knocked those men over like ninepins. But it never occurred to him to do so; he was not aware of his great strength. He had intended to take Anna to this dance, if only she had behaved differently towards him. He fingered the little parcel in his pocket. There was a necklace in it, a string of beads. It had been in his pocket since morning. The ache in his heart became unbearable; he involuntarily clenched his fist, the string snapped, and the beads came apart inside the parcel. No matter: they were no longer of any importance.

He might have got over it, if only she had ignored him altogether. But Anna would not let him be: she liked to irritate him. She would pass by with a provocative swagger and, if Ansis was near at hand, she would flirt outrageously with any man who happened to be there.

When the first hay was brought in to be stored, Anna was up in the hayloft with the other farmhand, taking in the stacks. Whenever there was a pause in the work the two of them frolicked and romped about as if they had taken leave of their senses.

Standing down below, with a pitchfork in his hand, Ansis heard Anna squeal. It was natural of her to make a great deal of unnecessary noise, even at work.

But he stood down below, massive and powerful, pretending not to care; then he dug his pitchfork into almost half a cartload of hay and tossed it into the loft as if it were a sackful of feathers. The farmer, who had appeared at that moment, flung up his arms in amazement, and the farmhand called out to Ansis from the hayloft to slow down a little — he couldn't manage such a load all at once.

Not a muscle stirred in Ansis' face; he made no answer and went on with his work. But now and then there was a sudden flash in his blue eyes, like a flame leaping up. From now on, try as she might, Anna could not provoke him into any rash, impulsive action whatever. This displeased her. She would have liked to see him groveling at her feet, helpless with love.

She sought ways and means of getting at his still smarting wound.

Apparently she had been talking about him. Even the lads from the neighboring farm smirked and asked him pointed questions. And then it happened that Anna, rummaging through his clothes, came upon the broken string of beads in the pocket of his best suit. The beads had been there ever since that Sunday.

She took them to the room shared by the farm people and, laughing, showed them to everybody; they all thought it a huge joke. Ansis snatched the beads from her and put them into his pocket.

"They weren't meant for you," he said.

Anna seemed to take offense.

"For me? Heaven forbid that I should let you give me a string of beads! Gracious me, such a grand present! No, I wouldn't let you ruin yourself for my sake!"

In this strain she went on and on, and everybody was helpless with laughter.

The joke about the beads was not allowed to rest. Not a day passed without someone's alluding to it. And one morning, while they were all raking hay, the other farmhand, taking a sip of water and wiping his mouth with his bare forearm, started again:

"What about those beads, Ansis? Whom did you want to give them? The girls can't make it out."

Ansis moved away to the other side of the meadow. But the chatter did not stop, and he heard them laughing — laughing at him . . .

At midday he walked across to the farthest haystack near the edge of the wood, and lay down.

The sun stood high above, casting a fierce white light over the mowed fields and the undulating lines of distant woods. Now and then, a drowsy little breeze sprang up among the clump of alders nearby, to subside almost at once. Beyond the grove, small clouds of smoke, barely discernible, rose like incense into the blue of the

43

sky. Very likely Anna was busy cooking. She would be all by herself; the others were out here in the meadow, taking their noonday nap.

A sudden resolution formed in Ansis' mind. He sat up and looked around. No one was paying any attention to him. He rose to his feet and walked with long strides straight through the grove and to the farmhouse.

He entered the kitchen so quietly that Anna, bending over the cookstove, did not hear him; she gave a start when she suddenly caught sight of him.

"Good heavens, what d'you think you're doing, slinking about like a thief, giving people a fright! What d'you want here, in the middle of the day . . . " She stopped abruptly.

His face wore a curious expression. There was a strange glitter in his wide, staring eyes, his face was flushed, and his hands were awkwardly fumbling with the open collar of his shirt as though he was not quite sure what he meant to do. He sat down on the very edge of a chair, as if just for a moment, as if he would have to get up again immediately and continue on his way. Thus he kept sitting there, his eyes on the floor, rubbing his big hands.

"I wanted to . . . about those beads . . . they were for you . . ."

She eyed him closely.

"What? You wanted to give those beads to me?"

He got up and suddenly caught hold of Anna by her bare arms, just above the elbows.

"Yes, that time . . . but they're all right, they can be strung again."

She saw the look of confusion in the young lad's face, and it struck her as very funny and childish. She was overcome with laughter, but could not open her mouth. Ansis had pulled her close to him and was trying to kiss her. Anna jerked her head downwards, and his mouth fell upon it with such violence that he hurt his teeth in spite of her thick hair. Nothing came of the kiss. She broke away from

44

his embrace and fingered the marks his fierce grip had left on her arms. They were white from the pressure of his hands, the blood returned only slowly, and now they became a mottled red. She was obviously upset about them.

"Leave me alone with your beads. Carrying on like a fool. Haven't even been in the army yet . . . You might as well chop some wood, since you're here anyway. The fire's gone out, too." She opened the door of the stove and threw in some wood shavings.

Ansis slowly picked up the ax and, for a while, stood there, deep in thought. He needed time to ponder what had just happened. At last he bent down beside Anna and began to chop wood on the flagstones in front of the stove. One blow of the ax followed another at exact intervals, cutting the log into pieces matched to a hair's breadth; with a quick swing, never releasing his grip on the wood, he finally brought the ax down along the very edge of the log. The white pieces of wood fell in a perfect row. He proceeded to chop them crosswise into small bits.

Anna raked the fire in the stove and threw in some large pieces of wood, shavings, and some of the kindling wood he had chopped for her.

Ansis took another log and raised the ax. As she was bending over the stove his eyes suddenly fell on the woman's white neck with its narrow line of suntan between blouse and hair. There was something unpleasantly sensuous about the whiteness of her flesh. He stood and gazed at the raised ax in his hand. Small blue sparks began to flicker in his eyes. He turned the ax slightly sideways and brought it down with full force.

The log lay there, untouched. But Anna gave a slight groan and collapsed. Her body twitched strangely in the agony of death. Then it was all over.

Ansis stood with the ax in his hand, thinking. His thoughts came very slowly; but once they got under way his mind worked methodically and to the purpose, like a good plough horse.

45

He glanced at the body on the floor, and turned away.

For him, all was not over yet. His mind pulled the heavy plough of his thoughts, seeking a solution for his predicament in the merrily crackling fire in the stove. Fire, too, was a destroyer.

Ansis went into the adjoining room and picked up a few pieces of clothing belonging to the farmer's wife and the dried-up birch sapling which had stood forgotten in a corner since it had been brought in to make the room festive for Midsummer Night. He put these things on a chair in the kitchen, piled some wood and shavings on top, and pushed some of the farmer's newspapers underneath. Then he fetched a can of paraffin from the storeroom, poured its contents over the pile he had made, and put the can back in its place.

The only thing needed now was fire. The door of the stove stood open, and Ansis could have got fire from there. But he would have had to reach across the body on the floor, and this was distasteful to him.

He found some matches and was just about to light one when an idea struck him. He went to get his Sunday suit, turned it over in his hands, undecided, and finally put it back on its peg. No, he was not so simple as he looked, this child of nature with his darkened soul.

He took only the beads and put them into his pocket. There was a slight trembling in his hands when he fingered the beads, but not for long.

Then he set fire to the things he had heaped on the kitchen chair and drenched with paraffin, and made for the door. Noticing the key in the lock, he took it and locked the door from the outside. Suddenly he changed his mind, unlocked the door, and re-entered the house. He was met by billowing smoke. Having locked the door from the inside, and leaving the key in the lock, he cautiously crawled out of the window which faced the wood. There was no one to be seen.

Drawing his head down between his shoulders, Ansis made a dash

46

for the wood and was soon back on the farther side of the meadow. All the farm people were still asleep.

He lay down at the foot of the same haystack as before. His eyes, blue as a child's, watched the clouds of smoke behind the copse grow denser and blacker while his hand kept playing with the broken string of beads in his pocket.

IN THE BLIZZARD

A SOUTHWEST wind had set in, developing into a blizzard that did not die down for two days; it flung a tangled mass of thick, wet snowflakes at everything that stood in its path, and howled with strange animal voices about the gables of the farm buildings. Krauklis, the owner of the farm, lay in the loft above the stable, wrapped in his fur coat; his unshaven chin was raised towards the little window let into the roof, and he listened with melancholy satisfaction to the voices of the wind. He would have liked it even better if their shrillness had increased, if they had grown crazier still and the raging storm had gathered such force that it carried off the roofs and himself, hurtling everything pell-mell, dashed to fragments, into the abyss of the universe.

True, the rafters creaked now and again, but Nature did not destroy man's handiwork this time and therefore did not help the farmer to solve certain problems that had to be solved by him alone. As a matter of fact, he had already decided how to set about it. It was not for nothing that he had been lying here in the loft since last night. Now he had only to come to terms with himself in his own heart, to summon his strength, and to keep a cool head. He did not want to be rash again. In the beginning he had lost control of himself. In his first shock, at the discovery of his wife's infidelity, he had gone too far; he had even hit her. He lamely tried to justify

48

himself: he had done it because she hadn't admitted her guilt right away. Yet he was ashamed of himself. It was impossible to keep this scene a secret from the others on the farm. But they had probably guessed things earlier than Krauklis himself: in such cases, the husband is one of the last to find out. Now fate had punished him for his pride and self-righteousness, for owning the swiftest horses, for having the most beautiful wife in the whole parish. Certainly he hadn't hit Ilze for the reasons he had yesterday flung in her face. With bitter self-torment he remembered that he had perversely reproached her for the very things in which he had formerly taken such pride.

He had not shrunk from reminding his wife that she was a poor schoolmaster's daughter, and from rebuking her for her good education. In the past he used to say: I'm rich myself, I don't need a wife with a dowry.

She was so refined! — and too delicate to do all the work which, according to the old, established view, it was right and proper for the mistress of the farm to take upon herself. Yes, he himself had said: My mother, who is dead now, had far too hard and bitter a life; I don't want my wife to suffer the same fate, I don't want her to become worn out and ugly with drudgery.

Ilze liked company, and she often drove to the nearby town where her godmother lived. Did she go there in order to meet farmer Varpa? That had been his accusation yesterday. But it wasn't true; no: she had various interests, she wanted to go to the theater, to buy new books, to meet people. No wonder that the company of the neighboring farmers did not satisfy her — old men who spoke about nothing but cattle, crops, prices, and taxes, and who, to make matters worse, reeked of vile tobacco and strong spirits. And farmer Varpa was a fine lad. Krauklis himself had taken a fancy to him. When Varpa had given up his job as ship's mechanic and had come to work the family's farm after his brother's death, a change had come over the place; it looked well cared for and much improved.

The man had seen the world, and Ilze was not the only one who had found it pleasant to have a chat with him.

Yes, when he thoroughly considered all he had said last night, he realized that he had upbraided his wife for the very things he had formerly regarded as his and her special privileges. Only everything had been twisted and distorted by the sudden onrush of his jealousy and hurt pride. He had shown the same kind of mind and had said the same things as his gossiping neighbors whose tales about him and his private life had occasionally come to his ears.

He shouldn't have done those things; particularly, he shouldn't have hit her! He sank into calm, soothing melancholy. If one looked at the whole matter more objectively, it assumed a different complexion: what he used to be proud of was perfectly sound; even now, in retrospect, there was nothing to be ashamed of, nothing to regret. True, his misfortune hurt him, but it was an ordinary everyday occurrence, a wife's falling in love with another man. Why? Well, why had he fallen in love with his wife? Why hadn't he married Alvine, the youngest daughter of his neighbor, Ezergailis? She was a quiet, hard-working girl, knowledgeable about cattle. After his wedding she had found work a few parishes further off; and people said she was so much in love with him that she would never marry. No doubt everyone on this earth has his share of sufferings. And now it was his turn.

Still, his wife ought to have told him sooner! As yet, they had no children — thank God! But farmer Varpa! Well, that would be the last straw! A deceived husband's fury again rose in him. But, after all, everyone is likely to take what is accessible. He himself knew that well enough. Now it was also clear why young Varpa, this high-spirited, fair-haired lad, had lately been so depressed and reserved in his presence and had even seemed to avoid him. Varpa had obviously felt uncomfortable: when one is in love with a man's wife one doesn't exactly enjoy her husband's company. Yes, now it was easy to see it all!

50

The most important decision still remained: to disentangle the knot, or cut it? That was why he had been lying in the loft since last night, thinking. Fight over it, divorce her, take her back? Objectively, it was quite a commonplace situation; faithless wives were nothing unusual in this world. But unfortunately it was his own wife this time! The farmer's characteristic pride and his hard, rather obstinate peasant mind could not be satisfied with a simple, unspectacular solution of the problem. He had always done things in his own way and had secretly smiled down his beard when others were puzzled and could not make out what he was going to do next. No doubt half the parish were already racking their brains, trying to guess how he would react to his misfortune. And this time, too, he would not allow his honor and pride to suffer. He had not been lying here above the stable since last night, carefully considering every aspect of the problem, merely to go and fight it out with Varpa; or to make his terrified wife swear she regretted her misdemeanor and would in future be virtuous; or to collect evidence for a court of law, evidence which would publicize his own shame and humiliation, and to start tedious divorce proceedings accompanied by gossip and tittle-tattle.

Neither did he want to do anything violent. He had loved his wife, and probably loved her still. Was it possible that he had been completely mistaken, that she had never been worthy of his love? No: everything he had done so far had been perfectly justified, and what he was about to do would be equally right. At the thought of it his mouth curved into a rather sly, superior smile in spite of the pang of sadness in his heart. Those two had not acted honorably. They would get what was coming to them! And how! They had brought shame upon him, and now they themselves would have good reason to be ashamed! Shame and disgrace would enter Varpa's farm. But, most of all, they'd be amazed! And, what was more, they wouldn't be the only ones to be amazed.

A door shut noisily down below. The bent, heavy figure of Jekabs,

51

the old farm laborer, loomed up through the trapdoor. Nervously groping about, he heaved himself up and stood sideways to Krauklis, trying to say something. Although the old man had carefully prepared many words in his heart, none of them would pass his lips; yet his eyes showed that he had resorted to a good deal of beer and spirits to bolster up his courage. Only a prolonged stammering escaped him: "Eh . . . master, I'd say . . . eh, what the . . . bad business! But one mustn't, like that . . . they're all like corpses in the house. One way or the other, but . . . you must come down!"

Well, well, the farmer thought, he had obviously ruined his people's Saturday night. No doubt they were fidgety, ill-tempered, their nerves on edge. They all knew that something more was bound to happen, and they were waiting for it. But what was it going to be? Nobody could foretell. The decision was here, with him, and he was going to act. The patience of the household was at an end. The old farm laborer himself was too awkward and slow-witted in matters that needed discussion, he had probably been egged on by his wife to go and find out what the master was up to.

He caught sight of the bottle peeping out of the old man's pocket, and he smiled. Encouraged by this, Jekabs drew nearer and threw himself down in the hay beside the farmer. "I thought, master . . . eh, one ought to have a bite of something!" And he produced two slices of bread and a piece of ham from the other pocket.

The presence of another human being brought the farmer back to the realities of life with all its odiousness. "Thanks, Jekabs!" He did not feel like eating but did not want to sadden the old man, and he accepted a slice of bread and bit into it. "No, no, leave it there," he refused the bottle of liquor which the farm laborer had timidly started to pull out of his pocket. "It will come in useful for yourself . . . on the road. There's some driving to be done. Feed the horses . . . the mare and the white one."

"A long way to go?"

"Not exactly."

"Eh . . . has something to be taken away to somewhere?"

"Yes, something has to be taken away! First you'll have to go by yourself, and then I'll go part of the way too," the farmer said, pushing the last and biggest morsel of bread into his mouth. Now the final decision was made, it would serve no purpose to delay any longer. All the household were waiting for him, no doubt his wife too. What a depressing Sunday, with no work to be done, and time hanging heavily on everybody's hands. . . . They were waiting, and now something was going to happen!

As Krauklis stepped out into the open the storm hurled masses of caked snow against his face and into his open fur coat. Holding himself erect, he slowly crossed the yard, making no attempt to protect himself from the blizzard — as though he wanted to draw strength from the forces raging about him, to steel himself for the task that lay before him. He stopped for a moment by the door, shivering, and then he entered the kitchen which was next to the livingroom shared by the farmhands. He greeted them in a loud voice and felt the gaze of five people leap to his face. It was only after a few moments that his greeting was returned by Jekabs' wife who stood leaning over the cookstove. The others remained silent, some with fright, some with surprise. The water could be heard bubbling in the large pot, and cockroaches made a rustling sound as they scurried about among the strings of onions hanging from the ceiling. The farmer crossed the room, and as he closed the door behind him he heard a sudden babble of excited voices. Jekabs must have entered, and they were probably pelting him with questions.

"Good afternoon!" he said as he entered the long, neatly white-washed room, the best in the house. But this time his voice did not ring out so loudly; he seemed slightly hoarse. After a short cough, he slowly pulled off his fur coat.

Ilze remained silent; she had given a start and had turned away from the cupboard, interrupting her packing. She looked at him, frightened. Her large blue eyes, usually sparkling with life, were reddened with weeping and the eyelids were swollen. Her white hand convulsively clutched at the open door of the cupboard, and the farmer noticed that she no longer wore her wedding ring; there was only a narrow mark around her finger where it had cut into the skin. She was dressed in a colored cotton frock and a blue hand-knitted cardigan: the very things she had worn before her marriage. She looked child-like and fragile, exactly like the schoolgirl she had been when farmer Krauklis first met her. For a moment he felt giddy, overcome with memories of a great love: the scent of summer meadows and woods, silent moonlight, the warmth of her small shoulders leaning against his chest. He sat down by the table, passed his hand over his face and tried to control his emotion.

He had lowered his eyes, and his glance traveled across the floor until it reached the chest of drawers at the far end of the room. There lay a half-open suitcase. He rose, walked heavily towards it, and looked at its contents: a few articles of clothing, some trifles, but mostly books. These were the things she had brought with her when she came to the Krauklis farm.

"You want to leave?" He half turned to his wife who had sat down on the edge of the bed, leaning forward, her elbows on her knees, her numb gaze fixed on her husband's broad figure bent over the suitcase.

"Yes . . . to go to town, to my godmother!" she answered, again with a start. "What else is there left for me to do . . ."

The farmer did not reply but turned away and again looked at the suitcase. He heard suppressed sobs behind him. His silence was obviously more than she could bear. Tortured with suspense, she was waiting for the decisive word. She was afraid of what her husband might say, as she had often been in the past. His words always came with an unexpected significance and heavy force. Even at moments of greatest happiness she had felt slightly frightened of this proud, taciturn man who was like a craggy mountain peak that looked grim even on the sunniest day. In his presence, Ilze had always suffered from a strange feeling of constraint. Even his laugh was harsh and startling. She remembered farmer Varpa's laughter; it was light and playful, and he had several ways of laughing — easy, unhampered sounds that rang out like loose coins chinking in one's pocket. Yes, with farmer Varpa one could talk about everything that entered one's mind, even about merest trifles, and he was always ready with a witty retort. But her husband sometimes did not answer at all, he merely smiled his inevitable smile of superiority.

She longed to be somewhere far away at this moment, no matter where, but somewhere surrounded by people; her spirit was broken, she was dead tired. She would drive to town, to her godmother, and try to find some sort of work. If only this man didn't again spring some surprise on her! He always devised something to test her with. Sometimes it was only a good-natured joke, but she was unnerved by the continual threat of sudden surprises. His words often had a double meaning — the surface meaning and the hidden, real one — and she had to rack her brains, often in vain, to understand him correctly.

"So be it," the farmer at last said abruptly, and Ilze stared at him with surprised, incredulous eyes when she heard these simple words. "You are going to leave. But not the way you expected," he continued, and Ilze turned faint with forebodings. "Yesterday I taunted you with your poverty. That was wrong of me. But you must understand and forgive me: you also haven't behaved as you should! We have both been rich these three years — rich in happiness, while it lasted. For this I thank you. I have really been happy, though it isn't in my nature to make a great show of it. That's one thing I wanted to say. The other is this: you are no longer a schoolmaster's daughter; you are the mistress of the Krauklis farm. It is impossible to step back into the past as one would step into an old frock. You must understand that! And therefore you shall leave as befits the mistress of a farm. I'll give you a portion worthy of your status."

55

"I don't want anything!"

"It is quite immaterial what you want or don't want! There are things that just have to be done. Perhaps I don't even want you to leave, but you'll have to, nonetheless!" He looked deeply, gravely into his wife's eyes, and she knew she had no strength to oppose him. Nobody on this farm could go against the master's wishes. She, too, was powerless to do so while she was still here. Very well, then: she would leave at a time and in a manner laid down by him. And when at last she got away, the spell this house cast over her would be broken. It lay heavily upon her; it was the first thing of which she had to rid herself.

"Come on, dress as befits the mistress of this farm! I'll send someone to help you with the packing . . ."

"No, please, anything but that! I'd much rather do it myself!"

Krauklis reflected for a moment. Clearly, his wife was ashamed, she could not face any of the household. He thought of what lay before her in the hours to come, and gave in. "All right. I'll only give orders for the boxes to be brought into the room next door, and I'll help you myself to get all the things together which you'll have to take with you. First of all, pack everything that has belonged to you all the time. And don't dawdle! I want you to leave before it gets dark."

He went into the adjoining room, almost cheerful: the first step was taken! He shaved, trimmed his beard, and gave orders for various chests and boxes to be brought, together with things that were not in daily use. Let people see how splendidly and richly provided his wife was leaving! Let them cudgel their brains, trying to make out what exactly was going on! Then he himself lent a hand at packing the blankets, bedspreads, lengths of hand-woven cloth, towels, tablecloths, even the alarm clock and the valuables she refused to take.

"Oh God! . . . What's all this for? Really, I don't need anything!" Ilze protested.

56

"I said I'd give you a proper dowry, and that's what I'm going to do. Besides, it will be to our credit in people's eyes."

"What's the good of it! Now — in our present circumstances!"

"You're wrong there! Our married life has come to an end, but not our lives — we cannot escape so easily as that. We'll have to go on living in the midst of people. Go on with your packing! We'll leave soon."

He went back to the adjoining room and started to write a letter. It was only a short note, but it required much thought and effort. Finally this, too, was done. He went out to the coach house.

Ilze sat down among the packages and boxes, and burst into tears. Her husband's generosity increased her feeling of guilt. After a while she rose again and examined the pile of luggage, rearranging and repacking a few things. And her eyes, still wet with tears, involuntarily took pleasure in what they saw. Beautiful, useful things, all of them, and jewelry, too. . . . Of course, she would never wear any of it again, no, never! Just this little silver brooch, perhaps. How it would sparkle on her cornflower-blue blouse! No, all the same, she wouldn't wear it. But if her husband wished it she'd take it with her. If only she could get away soon, if only it were soon over! Afterwards, she might return some of the things to him. . . . She still had to face the divorce — ugly, tormenting proceedings in a law court. How was she ever to endure it? And what was to happen to her afterwards, what would be left to her in life? She ought to consult farmer Varpa; she would need advice. Oh, the shame of it! What would he say about the whole thing? No, she couldn't bear to think of it. . . . Her kind, loving godmother! . . . She also was sure to be distressed. Oh, if only everything were soon over and done with, including the talking she had to do! And then, oh, to crawl into some corner where nobody came near her, nobody asked her any questions!

Jekabs was harnessing the white horse to the sledge when the farmer himself led his favorite, the black mare, out of the stable and harnessed her to his own richly ornamented sleigh. She snorted and tossed her mane in the whirling snow which blew in by the open door of the coach house. Her large dark-blue eyes gazed at him with a gentle, slightly playful expression, as is the way with a well-groomed carriage horse. Somehow, they reminded him of his wife's blue eyes which at times had the same playful look. He fondled the mare's soft, velvety lower lip which lay gently quivering in the palm of his hand like a warm, damp, newly captured mole, and again he felt the need to pull himself together and hurry if he wanted to carry out his plan. He had the boxes and suitcases loaded onto the sledge and told Jekabs to drive on ahead. He accompanied the old man for a short distance, gave him the letter he had just written, jumped off the sledge, and returned to the house.

"Well, so far so good! We're almost ready to start," Krauklis said to his wife as he entered the room. "But there's still a little time left. Now you must eat something."

"No, really, I don't feel hungry. . . . And the horse is waiting."

"Still, you'll have to eat! We'll sit here for a while," he insisted and gave orders for the table to be laid. His wife tried to eat some of the pie, but she put it back on her plate and gazed dumbly out of the window which was almost covered with caked snow. Slowly, deliberately, the farmer drank his coffee, occasionally glancing at the clock. When ten minutes had dragged out thus he could not bear the situation any longer.

"We'll go now!" he exclaimed, bringing his fist down heavily on the table. As though awakened from an evil dream, Ilze was sharply brought back to reality. Crying, she bent her head, and her legs did not obey her when she tried to rise. For the last time she had glanced through this window at the snow-covered garden with the well in the foreground and the blue, barely visible wooded hillock beyond in the distance. There she had wandered about, barefoot, in the summer, and bees were buzzing. . . . No — it was the wind, the blizzard. . . . Did she really have to leave? Perhaps, this very mo-

58

ment, she would wake up: was it a dream, or a bad joke? Her husband had become strangely pale, it even seemed as though his hands were trembling. Suddenly he was in a great hurry, he handed Ilze her fur coat and could hardly wait for the moment when she would tie the kerchief round her head and seat herself in the sleigh. Was he so anxious to be rid of her?

Ilze buried herself deeply in her fur coat and tried not to think. The farmer jumped into the sleigh from the other side, gave a pull at the reins, and suddenly they were already past the orchard and round the corner by the granary. A little bell, suspended from one shaft of the sleigh, kept up a crazy tinkling and jangling. Protecting herself from the blizzard, Ilze peeped at her husband from beneath a corner of her kerchief and was amazed to see him straining forward and urging on the mare, which needed no persuasion to go fast and had already broken into a gallop. Indistinctly, snow-laden bushes, willows by the roadside, and barns amid the fields flitted by like live things, swept on by fear and despair. Only the black mare's withers steadily rose and fell against a dark-grey background, the outline of the forest which dimly showed in the distance. The farmer saw none of these things; his eyes intently scanned the snow-covered road ahead, hoping to catch a glimpse of Jekabs with his leather cap, the flaps pulled down over his ears, and his head all muffled up. But the farmer had said to him: "Drive fast!" And now the farmer urged himself onwards, incessantly repeating the very same words. There could be no change in the situation if he did not catch up with the old farm laborer who had the letter, and he would have to complete the task he had set himself. He had lured his wife into a trap, but he was caught in it together with her; and now, with desperate haste, he tried to break free. At the moment, he could not imagine what would finally happen, but at least he would regain his freedom of action. Why had he been in such a hurry?! Wasn't it perhaps his happiness he was carrying away from his home, in a sleigh drawn through the blizzard by his swiftest horse?

By the time they reached the hillock, and came to the road that branched off to the Varpa farm, the blizzard had spent its force. The farmer's heart, too, filled with a profound, somber calm. Too late: here were the crossroads of his life. He stopped the horse, pulled at the reins, and the sleigh slowly turned into the road leading to the Varpa farm.

"Oh God! Where are you taking me?" Ilze moaned.

Krauklis turned to her, his snow-encrusted face had suddenly become hard and forbidding. "I wanted to . . . and I didn't want to. . . . But it was too late: we could no longer overtake Jekabs, he has already got there with the letter and your luggage. Forgive me. We'll have to go through with it, there's no other way!" He jumped off the sleigh and threw the reins to his wife. "You must drive on alone. May God help you! I can't — I can help neither you nor myself. Drive on, you must drive on!" he shouted, his mouth trembling and distorted, when his wife tried to stop the horse. "You're expected there!" He snatched up the whip, lashed out at the horse, and it flew down the hill at a gallop.

Krauklis stood motionless for a long time; fainter and fainter, the jingling of the sleighbell at last died away in the distance. Then he turned and slowly walked back towards his farm. The blizzard had subsided, and the soft, snowy contours of the countryside gained a fresh distinctness in the calm blue of the gathering dusk. There was peace and silence everywhere. All sound of the farmer's footsteps was smothered as he walked through the snowdrifts. Snow had obliterated the marks made by the sleigh: he had driven his happiness away and it had gone, leaving no trace.

In the meantime, farmer Varpa had given up questioning Jekabs about what exactly had taken place at the Krauklis farm and, providing him with food and drink, had made him sit down in the kitchen while he himself re-examined and re-read the letter for the hundredth time.

"Neighbor! I send you what you coveted — my wife. I am giving

60

her a dowry which, apart from the things Jekabs is bringing you, includes the sleigh and the black mare. I cannot act otherwise, and I hope that you will also act as befits a man of honor. The rest will be settled in court, though I do not feel like having much truck with it."

The young farmer alternately blushed and ruffled his fair curls. "Will it bring me happiness or unhappiness?" he whispered. "Everything must be received as honor demands!" Throwing back his head and smiling, he went out into the yard when the jingling of a sleigh-bell met his ears.

 **SILJONIS' JEWEL**

SILJONIS cast his fishing line into the Daugava, and a look of surprise came over his face when the float went down immediately only to pop up again as if the bait had been nibbled at by a small fish which lacked the strength to swallow it. He continued to jerk his line out and drop it in, humming to himself:

> He who hasn't got a thing
> Cannot deem himself a king,
> Nought but worries, woe and strife,
> Isn't this a hell of a life?

From the other side of the dock, old Gramba protested: "Don't sing so loudly, I nearly had a catch just now . . . Hello! Look out, your float's disappeared!"

Siljonis gave his line a jerk and landed a small bracelet with a glittering stone in its center.

"What is it?" asked Gramba.

"Don't know, must be something off a Christmas tree, though it's too early for that sort of thing." He turned the trinket round in his fingers until the water had dripped off it.

Gramba turned his head and gave it a look. "It's a diamond if it's anything!"

"You ought to know, you've ruined your mother-in-law . . ."
Siljonis laughed.

"It's a diamond all right!" Gramba placed the bracelet in the palm
of his hand. "Fifteen hundred lats at least — possibly more. How
fancy it looks!"

They had both dropped their fishing rods to look at the glittering
jewel.

The last rays of the sun slanted downwards through the gaps between the houses on the opposite bank, and the ripples on the water
were tinged with gold like the scales of fish; the little stone shone
like the brightest hope in their lives.

"We ought to report our find to the police," Siljonis said, hesi-
tating.

"Are you crazy? You'll be beaten and brought to trial!" Gramba
exclaimed angrily, with the authority of an expert. "And afterwards
you just try and prove that such things are caught with a line and
bait!"

"But some girl has lost it."

"Let her lose it if she wants to. And we have found it. Whoever
manages to lose such a thing isn't careful about anything at all and
therefore isn't really a loser. Are you sorry for the perch you pull
out? He is alive, with all his silver scales and golden fins. He's swallowed a hook — a disaster — but you, what are you doing? You
take his life without so much as feeling pity for him. I'll tell you why
I always make such poor catches: I'm just sorry for the fish!"

"You don't jerk your line at the right moment, that's what it is!"

"Perhaps, but then I can't stand the sight of them; my wife and
children eat them, I can't."

"Come now! Don't you eat pork either?"

"I eat cabbage when it's been cooked with pork, but I only pretend to eat the pork. There's always the fat; that's just as repulsive
to me as the meat. I have to eat something, though. But I loathe
eating altogether."

63

"I know . . . they reproach you."

"They always reproach me. . . . But if you've had the luck to pull out a diamond like this, to which no life is attached — what are you bothering about? Tomorrow we'll be rich. We'll sell it. I know the places where my mother-in-law goes to sell odds and ends. So don't worry!"

Gramba wound his line and Siljonis did the same, carefully wrapping the trinket in his handkerchief and putting it into his pocket.

"And now — have you got a lat?" Gramba asked.

"I've got two," Siljonis fumbled in his pockets, for the sake of appearances.

"A bottle of gin and two beers at the Old Dragon," Gramba decided, striding along resolutely. "Tomorrow we'll go to a smarter place, but for the time being we'd better keep quiet. There's no need to shout about one's good luck; it might take wings and fly away!"

They entered a riverside tavern where the tobacco smoke was so dense that it looked as though some of the customers' bald heads were covered with hair again. It was only by puffing hard to dispel the smoke that one could make out the person sitting opposite him at the table.

Gramba gulped down a glassful and cheered up.

"You know, people always look better if you're in a cheerful frame of mind yourself, but if you're not — they seem to be nothing but scoundrels and tipplers! Every one of them looks as if he thinks himself a prince! I've always wondered how on earth the Devil manages to make the round of all the churches and bars on one single night. He couldn't do it without assistants. But then there are the jealous wives who'll lend him a hand; they're always on the spot to help him. They'll be there to meet you, they're like veritable gates of terror you must pass. Which may give you a pretty accurate idea of the misery in store for you when you enter the true gates of hell."

"But perhaps they are only there as a warning," Siljonis laughed.

"A warning of what? Of the very Devil's jealousy, eh? While you

64

are still able to cast glances at other girls, you are a wicked man; and when you end up caring for nothing but boiled cabbage they'll grudge you even that. You must not eat cabbage, for some of your love goes into eating it; l-o-v-e — what an all-embracing word! You may interpret it as you please. You must not leave the house by the main door, for you may come to like it. You may begin to love that door, too! You mustn't catch too many fish, for you may come to love catching fish."

The gin gradually disappeared down Gramba's gullet, like grain in a government grain elevator.

"Do you really think it is a diamond?" Siljonis asked, also slightly tipsy.

"Don't you worry about that, I've seen lots of them!" Gramba assured him.

They were longshoremen, both of them, but because of a strike they had been out of work for two weeks. Unable to hit upon anything more sensible, they had taken to angling. In addition, their wives kept dinning into their ears that they should be out and doing something.

On reaching Gramba's house, Siljonis pushed him in through the door. Then, slightly apprehensive, he proceeded toward his own abode.

His wife did not like his being in Gramba's company at late hours; he crossed his threshold feeling like a martyr. The children were asleep; his wife was not. She turned the bedside lamp on him and eyed him for a while, but she didn't say a word.

He put away his fishing rod, washed himself, and lay down. The light was turned off, but he could not sleep.

Fifteen hundred lats! he thought. A bicycle for his boy, and for his wife anything she might wish for. Actually, what would she really want to have? A hat, a dress, a coat, furs, a new flat? There would not possibly be enough money for all that. And Gramba needed a new jacket. How could he forget that? First and foremost, he would

65

buy a jacket for Gramba, then a bike for his boy, and afterwards he would see if for his wife . . . Oh, there would be enough left for her too! The way she'd open her eyes wide, not knowing what to buy first! How he would like to give her this surprise . . .

If the diamond brought in, say, five hundred lats or even only a hundred lats. . . . But then again it was a thing he had found; it had to be reported. But wasn't Gramba right: if a girl managed to lose such a thing, of what value could it really be to her? He got angry with himself and fell asleep.

The next morning he took his fishing rod and asked his wife for a lat from their common funds.

"This catching fish of yours costs us more money than your staying at home would," she remarked, handing him the lat.

"And you'd certainly look much nicer if you worried less," he waved one hand at her while the other felt for the trinket in his handkerchief.

They met at the dock, and Gramba examined the ornament narrowly. "Do you know," he said, "the stone doesn't look so transparent to me as it did yesterday. I hope we haven't been mistaken! But surely we'll get *something* for it!"

They set out briskly for a basement shop in the old part of the city.

"It is a bit of cut glass," a dark-haired youth informed them there, looking at the trinket and holding it up against the light that came through the basement window.

"But it must be a piece of very good glass!" Gramba was trying to hold his ground.

The young man smiled and looked at the jewel through a black-framed magnifying glass. "It is indeed a piece of very good glass, as you said, Mr. Gramba."

"Well, now you see what they are beginning to wear instead of genuine precious stones! There's no relying on anything any longer!" Gramba said indignantly to Siljonis.

66

"Will you give me a lat for it?" he appealed to the dark-haired youth.

"I'm sorry, but we don't buy this sort of thing, Mr. Gramba." The youth waved his hands with a negative gesture, accompanying it with a regretful smile.

They left and walked towards the riverside with their fishing rods. Siljonis in silence, Gramba talking. "Now, look, what harm did the catching of this jewel really do us? You came to a compromise with your conscience — and I, well, I once more realized that I haven't got such a thing as a conscience at all. Now that we know how cheap this trinket is we no longer talk about reporting it to the police. . . . But who knows, girls may still set some value on things they lose, small as they may be . . ."

All of a sudden, Siljonis grasped Gramba by his collar and laughingly began to choke him. "Tell me, you old ragamuffin, you knew all along that it was just an ordinary piece of glass, didn't you?"

"I didn't, really . . . wait . . . let go . . . I thought it might be glass, but then I thought I might be mistaken. . . . Anyhow wasn't it a lovely evening?"

"Yes, but the morning wasn't pleasant at all." Siljonis let Gramba's collar go.

"Mornings never are," Gramba reasoned, smoothing his collar. "When you have to work they are too far from the evening, and when you sleep they are too soon after the night."

They sat down on the dock and cast their lines. Siljonis pulled out a perch and threw it over to where his friend was sitting, for the latter rarely succeeded in catching anything. In this way he was really catching fish for two. His wife despised him for this unprofitable friendship.

But when he looked at this man to whom life had brought nothing but failure and who always sought to trick him with some momentary glittering illusion, he somehow felt sorry for him and wished once more that he could buy him a new jacket.

67

He would never be able to save enough money for that, and the needs of his own family always came first.

"But if ever I have the money, I'll certainly do it!"

This was what held them together. And that night, Siljonis, as usual, spent his lat at the pub, for Gramba was his jewel, a jewel bright, unique, and good for nothing.

THE FIERY DESCENT OF OLD KORIS

AN OLD Latvian saying has it that the Devil wears out nine pairs of shoes before he brings two young people together in marriage. We do not know the Devil's requirements as to footwear — though they are probably exacting if he wishes to be present wherever his name is mentioned. On the other hand, it is common knowledge that shortly before his wedding Juris Akots performed a feat of running that would have done credit to the Devil himself.

But that is not the beginning of the story. In the beginning, everything went smoothly and pleasantly. Juris, the younger son of miller Akots, had returned from doing his military service. He met Anda Koris in the cemetery on the annual feast day in commemoration of the dead. From the way they looked at each other, it was not difficult to guess what this encounter was going to lead to. Masses of flowers in all their summer glory bedecked the resting places of the departed; yet, in that very place, two young people smiled at each other as though all this transience overshadowed by graveyard crosses were nothing very serious.

After that day it became clear that Anda's other suitors would be merely wasting their time. They ought to have scattered like last year's leaves before the vigorous breezes of spring. If they did not do so at once it was only because they were heavier and more tenacious than leaves. Some young men persisted in encountering Anda in the road, as though by accident, and involving her in conversation, although the girl's noncommittal replies made it difficult to converse at any length, and her preoccupied air showed that in her thoughts she was walking somewhere else — with someone else. Such was the change which in a few summer weeks had come over the prospects of the lads who wooed the beautiful heiress of a prosperous farm.

It still remained to be seen what old Koris, Anda's father, would have to say about the matter. He was a brisk, rosy old fellow with white mustaches which sometimes acquired quite a jaunty angle, especially when he had occasion to sit rather long over his beer and brandy. Well, old Koris said nothing. Or rather he said a great deal, for he was a talkative, friendly soul; but he never once alluded to this particular subject.

The more simple-minded of the rebuffed suitors tried to wreck Juris's chances by acquainting old Koris with the women's tittle-tattle about the young man's wild debaucheries during his military service. He listened with his usual affability, and in the end he remarked: "Well, well! Who would have thought it!"

The more crafty ones tried to draw him out by praising Juris's manly bearing and his capacity for hard work, to which old Koris replied simply by repeating their own words. His wife was dead, and for this reason the womenfolk of the parish, eminently experienced and shrewd judges in such matters, were unable to employ their talents to the full: there was nobody with whom to establish contact.

Miller Akots, too, was a complete loss: he also was a widower; besides, he suffered from some chronic internal complaint, spending most of his time upstairs in bed, and the morose look in his face did not encourage any questioning. Because both his sons worked diligently at the mill and were on the best of terms with each other, it was no use hoping for a rupture within the family by which one might have gleaned something.

70

Attentive observers would have noticed that his daughter's pre-occupation did not strike old Koris as a matter to be taken lightly. Whenever Juris entered or left a room the old man's eyes momentarily rested with close, earnest scrutiny on the lad's supple figure and bright, open face. He sometimes even broke off in the middle of one of his funny stories and listened carefully to every word, every chance remark Juris dropped in passing. Nothing unpleasant ever met his ears or eyes: Juris's voice rang out clearly, his words were to the point, and his jokes brief and apt — exactly the kind he could permit himself at his age. He did not avoid drinking and never spoiled the general conviviality with hateful temperance or precipitate departure; nor was he ever among those who lingered on in a state of maudlin drunkenness, for he always found a good excuse for getting away in time.

In a word, everything about Juris seemed all right. This must have been the conclusion reached by Koris after his careful observations; because Juris was given a hint to the effect that he would be expected at the Koris farm on the evening of the old man's birthday. Usually only the oldest and nearest neighbors were invited on this great day, and therefore the hint to Juris was no ordinary invitation and was not worded as such.

On the birthday, after breakfast, Anda asked who the visitors were going to be. Her father said briefly: "The same old friends, as usual." But, turning round just as he reached the door, he added: "And Juris, perhaps." The girl blushed scarlet with surprise. "Did you invite him?"

"As if I ever invited anybody! Whoever comes is welcome!" Old Koris quickly left the room. His daughter did not question him any further; but at midday she ran to the mill as fast as her legs would carry her and told Juris about the conversation with her father. They decided that it was essential for him to appear in the evening, for the old man probably thought the time had come for Juris to take more decisive action. Because of this, Juris set out for the Koris farm that night with a tremulous heart, though he was by nature courageous.

He arrived in the early evening. There was a great din going on in all the rooms and the garden; the old fellows had already been celebrating for a while. Furthermore, as one of them said, they had neither eaten nor drunk since the previous evening. They had only tossed a few grains of salt into their mouths every now and then — to work up a powerful thirst.

Juris did not want to give the impression that because of Anda his position was different from that of the other guests, and he therefore kept away from her. But the others were not slow to guess the real reason for the young man's presence. As the drinks mounted to their heads they increasingly felt the urge to have a heart-to-heart chat with the prospective son-in-law and to drink with him. And this they did, each in turn.

At length, Juris was being pulled and pushed about in all directions. He was tugged by his sleeves and slapped on the back. He had to listen to everybody and drink with everybody. Again and again he tried to slip away among guests who were leaving, but old Koris detained him every time, asking him some question or making him open a fresh bottle. The old man's eyes sparkled, his rosy face beamed, and his mustaches stuck out as dashingly as a Czarist dragoon's, which was not surprising: he had served in a cavalry regiment in the First World War.

The drinks mounted to Juris's head, too; he became bolder and more talkative, and he felt quite at home when Anda gave him furtive caressing glances or pushed some particularly tasty dish across to him. Warm night air and the scent of meadow grasses poured in through the open windows. The light bulbs spread a friendly glow, sometimes dimly gleaming through the clouds of tobacco smoke, sometimes sending out a bright shaft of light which came to rest on some old fellow's red nose. The guests became fewer, the conviviality increased.

72

Again, some visitors took their leave. This time Juris had managed to say good-by to Anda, snatching a quick kiss from her behind a door, but again old Koris detained him. Now there were only four of them left: Koris, two old farmers who had been his boyhood friends, and Juris.

For the last time, Anda tidied the table, arranged the remaining snacks on plates, and joined the men. But the old farmers' conversation was becoming so free and easy that she withdrew to her room and went to bed. The guests continued talking volubly but disconnectedly, paying little attention to each other's words but greatly admiring each other. Finally it happened that Juris found himself alone with old Koris. The farmer who had mentioned the grains of salt had fallen asleep at the end of the table; the other old farmer had gone out into the garden and vanished without anyone's taking the slightest notice.

Now was the moment to go home, but old Koris would not hear of it. He had become communicative and rather boastful. He talked so much that Juris could barely put in a word, though he tried to hint at what was nearest his heart. Old Koris began to discuss the management of his farm and produced a roll of paper from behind the cupboard: the plan of his farm. This was a great moment! The plan had been drawn by a relative of his, a surveyor, and it was a beautiful piece of work. Juris had heard that this plan was usually produced when old Koris had reached the height of blissful intoxication, and that he showed it only to his most intimate friends. Now the two of them examined and discussed it while they drank glass after glass, keeping strict pace with each other.

Red and green lights began to dance before Juris's eyes — a condition not entirely the result of the fact that fields, meadows, and woods on the plan seemed to have got all mixed up long ago. Now and then, everything was shrouded in yellowish smoke out of which there would emerge suddenly, threateningly, old Koris's huge brown pipe or his grand mustaches.

Juris summoned all his courage — now was the moment to put his cards on the table. He alluded to Anda. Koris cut him short, saying: "Not now! Another time!" And Juris was satisfied: this was sufficient for one evening, it was a step in the right direction.

"Well, it must be quite late, but wait a moment — I'll see if I can find some more beer, for a last drink!" Snatching up a jug, Koris disappeared into the darkness of the night, and Juris was left to himself. Perhaps his sense of time was slightly muddled, or old Koris was really staying away interminably; Juris began to feel bored and, worse still, overcome with drowsiness. Suddenly he remembered his father's advice which he had always followed: "If things are getting too much for you pick up your cap and make a dash for the door! A man of honor sleeps off his drunkenness at home."

In his present condition, Juris's head was incapable of forming more than one thought at a time; therefore, intent upon his father's advice, he suddenly jumped to his feet and left the house, completely forgetting old Koris. But when he walked through the garden and inhaled the fresh air it struck him that he ought to say good-by to his host. He turned back and listened by the door of the cellar where the barrel of beer was stored, but everything was dark and silent there. Then he looked through the window of the room, but there was no trace of old Koris; only the sleeping farmer was there, beginning to stir and yawn. Juris thought that Koris in his drunken stupor had perhaps wandered off somewhere to take a nap; in any case, there was still a visitor left who could take Juris's place. He was again overcome by such a longing for peace and sleep that he briskly set out for home along the moonlit road, trying to correct his uncertain balance by working up considerable speed.

It was a beautiful night, warm and silent, and the young man's heart was full of hopes and his sleepy eyes full of stars. He had been walking for about ten minutes when he suddenly heard the noise of a galloping horse's hoofs behind him. In the silence of the night, the sound seemed mysterious and rather frightening. Juris turned round

74

and stopped for a moment. The din grew louder, and from around a bend in the road there appeared a horseman enveloped in a pale cloud of dust.

Juris thought he was seeing a ghost: it was Koris, galloping along on his powerful black horse. The old man rode without a saddle, but he kept his seat splendidly, gripping the animal's flanks with his knees, his body bent forward, his white hair and mustaches streaming out in the wind; he looked like a horseman out of a fairytale. He stopped his horse with a jerk when he reached Juris, his bushy eyebrows bristling and his face full of ill-concealed fury.

"That won't do at all, guest of mine — only thieves slink away without a good-by! What's been put on the table has to be drunk. Jump up behind me, we'll ride back!"

Juris was suddenly quite sober. For a moment he almost laughed at the old man's crazy idea; then he realized with a shock the extent to which he had unwittingly annoyed Koris. He must have touched some very sensitive spot. Old Koris was universally lauded for his friendliness and sociability, but he was equally well known as a man of a very fiery temper. It was not for nothing that some people called him Mad Koris. Yes, Juris remembered it now. He had to try and make it up with him. What wouldn't one do for the sake of a girl!

"Yes, it's true, Koris, everything has gone wrong. I thought you went off to have a rest, but I see I was mistaken. Still, must I really take my punishment on the back of a horse, of all things? Haven't I perhaps deserved greater punishment than that? You've been so hospitable, I've felt so beautifully drunk all the evening, thanks to your generosity! But if we went back for that last drink of beer — wouldn't this wonderful feeling evaporate? It is more difficult for us both to ride on the same horse than to sit at the same table."

Koris's eyes flashed with rage. "Nothing doing, my lad! Difficulties when one's at work or difficulties when one's a guest — both have to be faced, otherwise there's no virtue in it!"

Juris saw that it would be dangerous to annoy the old man still

75

more, and he gave in. "Well, the back of the horse is sure to suffer in the cause of virtue! But what must be, must be." He shook himself and made ready to mount the horse. But Juris had never served in the cavalry as the old man had; his dealings with horses had been in broad daylight, when he was sober, and he had always tackled them from the front; now it required all his skill merely to climb up on the animal's smooth hindquarters. Koris dug his heels into its sides; the horse reared, almost throwing them both off, and broke into a mighty canter. Many a time, to keep his seat, Juris had to embrace the father more ardently than he had ever embraced the daughter.

Tired, completely sober, he soon sat at the table he had left only a short while ago. The old farmer who had been asleep was quite sprightly again and gave Juris a cheerful wink. It was obviously no secret to him in what manner Juris had been brought back to the table. After a while, the farmer who had disappeared also turned up: he had been taking a nap in the barn. A fresh jug of beer stood on the table, but Juris had lost all taste for it. The conversation flagged; Koris sat stiffly and gloomily on his chair. Clearly he would not be easily mollified.

When the jug was almost empty old Koris himself drank the last swallow, set the jug down on the table with a loud crash, and said: "I don't like to detain any guest who's in a hurry to be off."

"I'm not in a hurry, Koris, but I'll have to go home all the same." Juris tried to take his leave calmly and quietly, realizing that neither apologies nor explanations would serve any purpose. The two old farmers smirked and winked at each other. Koris testily shook hands with him and accompanied him to the door.

"Who has come by request leaves by request!" he growled mysteriously, giving Juris unpleasant food for thought which lasted him all the way home.

Thus ended the day that had begun so joyfully. Juris was very soon aware that something had happened which even his ride on

76

the black horse had not set right. Old Koris no longer took the slightest notice of him, and Anda was quite frightened and unable to give Juris advice. Finally he decided to take his courage in both hands, call on the old man, and have a very firm and serious talk with him — no matter what the outcome might be. But, just as he had made up his mind, various unpleasant rumors began to fly around which wounded his pride so deeply that he dismissed all thoughts of a reconciliation.

Koris's two old friends, who had witnessed the events of that fateful evening, had been unable to keep their mouths shut. That crazy ride through the night to fetch back the guest who had absconded, and the manner of his return, seemed too glorious a joke to keep secret. People admired the old man's tremendous hospitality and the zest with which he stood up for its laws. Juris, on the other hand, became a laughingstock; people said that in his drunkenness he had spent more time underneath the horse's belly than on its back, that he had continually climbed up and fallen off, and had in the end run behind the horse, holding on to its tail. While the story traveled from mouth to mouth it became so colorful that it was sheer joy to listen to, and it was spread even by those who wished Juris no harm.

People also repeated a powerful remark made by old Koris. That night, after all those annoying happenings, the two farmers had again drunk large quantities of beer with old Koris, and one of them had asked whether the new son-in-law was soon coming to live at the Koris farm. Thereupon, the old man had turned quite pale with rage (according to other versions, he had turned blue or purple), brought his mug of beer down on the table with a resounding clatter, and roared: "Son-in-law, what son-in-law? Even if he could catch up with me on foot when I'm on horseback, why, even then he wouldn't become my son-in-law!"

Juris suffered in silence, clenching his fists. He began to think of leaving his father's mill and looking for work somewhere farther away. Anda, unable to bear it any longer, approached her father

77

about the subject. Old Koris admitted that he had said something similar to what people were repeating, and, since he had said it, he was going to stick to it.

Autumn came, and those three people had still found no solution to the deadlock which had been brought about by such unfortunate circumstances. Perhaps old Koris regretted his rash words, perhaps he felt sorry for his daughter. Be that as it may, he had lost much of his former cheerfulness and was no longer seen in taverns and other places where the people of the parish habitually met to settle various matters of business.

Old Koris left his farm only when something particularly urgent had to be attended to. Among other things, he had to take his wool to the neighboring town to be woven into cloth. Time had slipped by, and he could not afford to delay any longer. Therefore, toward the end of November, the old man got ready to go to town. It was a dry, frosty morning, with the sun sparkling overhead. He had put the sacks of wool and some fodder for the horse into the cart; snugly wrapped up in his fur coat, he lit his pipe and gave the reins a leisurely tug. Needing no encouragement, the horse went off at a brisk trot, and the wind whistled past Koris's ears and chilled his face.

The road led over the top of the hill and then plunged down towards Akots's mill, continuing past a cluster of houses, including the grocer's and the chemist's. The space in front of the mill was crowded with people and carts; boys with skates and homemade sledges swarmed over the big frozen lake.

It was a Saturday, and the lively scene, bright with the glitter and sparkle of sunlight, surrounded by trees silvery with hoarfrost, made a picture it was a joy to behold. From the top of the hill, old Koris gazed at it with pleasure and then gave the horse full rein. The cart flew downhill, rattling and clattering on the frozen road. Koris saw that the crowd of men and boys had interrupted their sport and were looking at something, pointing and gesticulating. Some of them even shouted to him, probably to draw his attention to something unusual. At the speed he was traveling, the wind made such a noise in his ears that he could not hear what they shouted.

He smiled, gave them a cheerful wave of the hand, and continued on his way, peacefully puffing at his mighty pipe, quite unaware that his teeth were gripping the very object which was causing all the commotion. The string round one of the sacks of wool behind him had come undone, the wind had blown a few sparks from the pipe into the sack, and the wool had begun to smolder. When old Koris sped downhill, fire shot out from the back of his cart, and his rapid progress fanned the flames still higher. With a cheerful smile on his face, he came careering down the hill like the Prophet Elijah descending in his fiery chariot, leaving a long column of smoke in his wake and filling all beholders with confusion and wonderment.

Aware that Koris had either not heard them or had not understood what they were shouting, the crowd of spectators looked on helplessly, jostling and pushing each other and talking at the tops of their voices. Attracted by the noise, Juris had come out of the mill just as Koris drove past, merrily waving to the crowd. With bulging eyes, utterly bewildered, he watched the old man's progress. It was a sight both strange and comical. The boys shouted: "Koris, Koris, your bottom's on fire!" and Juris joined in the general laughter, undecided whether Koris's position was dangerous or merely funny. But he quickly checked himself — it was not becoming for him to laugh at a man who had made such a laughingstock of him. People might think he rejoiced at the old man's predicament. Besides, the whole cartload might catch fire and Koris himself come to grief. The horse might get out of control when it noticed the fire and smoke, and run away with the cart. There was no time to be lost; something had to be done at once. Yet there was no hope of catching up with the cart by running after it.

The road circled one side of the lake before it straightened again and entered the wood on the other side. It might have been possible to catch up with Koris by running straight across, but the middle of the lake was covered with only a thin sheet of ice; besides, hardly any snow had yet fallen to provide a foothold. Another possibility was to run round the lake in the opposite direction; here, the curve of the shore was much slighter, and the distance was shorter to the point where the road turned away to enter the wood. But the ground was very uneven, there were patches of reeds in many places, and anglers had trodden deep tracks down to the edge of the lake during the summer. Juris remembered this only after he had already started running. He was followed by a number of boys who yelled: "Koris, Koris, your cart's burning!" They were obviously determined that the event should lose none of its uproarious fun and should be duly accompanied by great noise and commotion. But Juris ran as if his whole life's happiness depended on it, and the boys were soon left behind.

One of the bystanders remarked: "The race is on — if Juris wins he'll be the son-in-law yet!" All the people living in the neighborhood of the mill had now assembled. In the unfortunate affair of the old man's birthday party, they had all been on Koris's side. But a sudden exciting event can completely reverse people's opinions, and now the whole crowd backed Juris; even those who had laughed at him now wished him success. Some of the more enterprising onlookers jumped into their carts and raced after Koris, shouting to their horses and lashing out with their whips. Others climbed the hillock to have a grandstand view of the proceedings, as though it were some big sporting event. The younger ones chanted words of encouragement to help Juris along.

Juris ran, intent upon taking the shortest possible route, bounding over the tufts of sedge which protruded from frozen inlets of water, and keeping an eye on Koris's smoking cart which was gradually drawing nearer to the part of the road that turned into the wood. His legs hurt; his breath began to give out. Leaping across a deep ditch, he misjudged the distance to the sedge that grew on the opposite

80

bank and took a heavy fall, breaking through the ice and bruising his hands and face. He was up to his waist in ice cold water, but the shock of it restored his energy. He scrambled out and threw off his jacket, realizing that he ought to have done so at the start. Around a curve of the lakeshore he saw Koris's cart approaching the point where the road turned away into the wood. Two carts in pursuit of Koris were by now even with Juris on the opposite shore.

The possibility of another humiliation roused Juris to fierce defiance. There was some snow on the part of the lake that still separated him from Koris, and he noticed that the ice had rather a rough surface because it had mingled with the snow when thawing. His fall had cost him about half a minute, he was in no position to lose any more time, and with a desperate effort he sprinted across the lake and along the road to meet Koris.

At last Koris had noticed him. He stopped his horse, and the two men met in the middle of the crossroads, at the very point where the old man would have turned off into the wood. Koris blinked with amazement when he saw the state Juris was in. "Always in a mess, Juris, that's what you are, always in a mess," he growled disapprovingly. No doubt he would have added a few penetrating remarks drawn from his fund of philosophical sayings if he had not been cut short by the smell of burning wool and the strange heat he suddenly felt at the seat of his fur coat. The moment the cart stopped, the horse had become aware of the fire behind it; snorting with fear, its nostrils extended, it plunged forward. Juris, gasping with lack of breath, leaped to meet it and hung on to the bridle. Now the two men drove up who had raced after old Koris; they flung the smoldering sacks of wool out of the cart and rolled them about in the snow by the edge of the wood. Some of the sacks were still intact.

Old Koris examined his fur coat into which the fire had burnt quite a sizable hole at the back. "Curse this strong tobacco," he exclaimed, realizing how the whole trouble had started. "I'd have ended up with smoking my whole cart away, and myself, too!"

81

"Will you be going to town, Koris?" Juris finally asked. Grinning, the other two men turned their carts round on the crossroads and made ready to drive away.

"Doesn't look like it. What's the use!" Old Koris glanced at the blackened sacks which filled the air with a revolting smell of burned wool. Juris took the horse by the bridle and turned Koris's cart; then he walked away in the direction of the mill. The old man drove after him. "Come, step in, I'll take you there!"

"I came here on foot, and I'll go home on foot," Juris said lightly.

Old Koris jumped off the cart and started to walk beside him. "In that case," he said, "I'll go on foot, too." And he added significantly: "There always seems to be some trouble with that horse." They looked gravely at each other; but they could not control their secret mirth, and suddenly they both smiled and burst into peals of laughter.

Thus the Devil did not wear out his nine pairs of shoes after all. Perhaps he had grown lazy in his old age and had therefore arranged matters in such a way that Juris had to do all the running instead.

"So you've escaped a fiery death, Koris! Did your soul get a taste of hellfire? You're hanging on to that runner of races, are you?" Amid such witticisms, flung at him unsparingly by the crowd which had collected in the yard, old Koris entered the mill with Juris. People continued standing there for a long time, gossiping about the two of them. An hour later, when they both reappeared, Juris was dressed in his Sunday suit, and they stepped into the cart and drove away to the Koris farm.

"Oh yes, that son-in-law caught up with the old fellow all right!" people said, laughing. A new story began to fly around, and while it traveled from mouth to mouth it became so colorful that even the participants found it sheer joy to listen to.

THE SECRET

ANNINA, six years old, the little daughter of farmer Askis, was drowned. Nobody had been with her at the time, nobody understood how it could have happened. Toward evening, when her mother was busy in the cowshed, people had seen her in the yard. When darkness fell they began to look for her; and by midnight they found her where the lake was deep, at the end of the little jetty, not far from the boat. Perhaps the child had wandered off on her own until she eventually came to the jetty, perhaps she had wanted to pick a waterlily which could be reached from the end of the boat — and then it had happened. . . . There was no other explanation.

It was one of those misfortunes that have to be accepted in silence, and to which the mind can find no approach. The only words the parson could say to the parents at the funeral were: Support each other with your love while you bear the burden of this affliction. And this they strove to do. They still had a little boy of three.

But their neighbor, Edvarts Lenums, seemed to be even more grief-stricken than the parents. He was married to Velga, the beautiful cousin of Askis's wife; they had no children of their own, and Edvarts had attached himself to Annina with the gentle tenderness that sometimes wells up in the hearts of people who have no one to give their love to, and who refuse to grow embittered and withdraw into themselves.

Life had turned out to be rather different from what it had seemed ten years ago when the two young farmers, having fought for the freedom of their country in the First World War, were each given part of the land that had formed an estate by the lake, and when they had fallen in love with the two cousins or, more exactly, with one of them — Velga. People still gossiped about the occasion when Edvarts had given his rival's head half an hour's ducking in the lake, and how he had only at intervals allowed him to gasp for breath, and had made him swear to keep out of the way. Maybe all this had been quite unnecessary. Everybody found it only natural that Edvarts, being more dashing and spirited than his rival, should win the more beautiful of the two girls. Askis accepted his fate and married Austra who was quieter and rather more ordinary. Afterwards, the neighbors were on good terms. But Velga had no children.

Now each had his own share of unhappiness, and neither seemed to have deserved it. But the misfortune that had overtaken his neighbor affected Edvarts just as much: Annina had been his godchild and the darling of his heart. Scarcely a day had passed without him calling on Askis and his family.

He had long since ceased to look at his wife when she went by, slim, graceful, with unfathomable dark eyes, perhaps even more attractive than she had been as a young girl, and still in the habit of wearing a flower in her black hair. She was herself like a strange flower, continuing in full bloom; but everybody had given up admiring her, except for strangers who happened to pass through that neighborhood. Austra, on the other hand, had become drab and shapeless; she had lost the small share of fresh, girlish beauty she had once possessed. She was a mother; this was clear at the first glance, and nobody gave her a second thought. But Edvarts felt during moments of quiet reflection that he had all too lightly passed something by, and that it had served no purpose to give Askis's head

84

a ducking in the lake. Yes, though it might seem harsh, he thought, this was the punishment for his youthful prank. It would not be true to say that he no longer loved his wife. But this love had become a heavy weight, and there were times when it gave them pain. It was possible to find forgetfulness in its passion, but there were many moments of emptiness when they found they had nothing to say to each other.

After the accident Edvarts no longer felt at ease with his neighbors. He spent a few evenings with them, and he brought Annina's toy home with him. It was a durable old toy — a red wooden pear with a little stem; it was hollow, and there was something inside that rattled when one shook it. He smiled sadly and put it on his table, and there it remained. Sometimes he even forgot to look at it, sometimes he picked it up and shook it to hear it rattle — not very often, only when he was in the mood to do something sentimental and slightly silly.

One day the toy disappeared from the table. Edvarts eventually found it, hidden away in a drawer. He put it back in its usual place. He merely put it down; he did not make it rattle for he had noticed that at such times his wife gave him a strained, searching look. He felt rather self-conscious about having taken a fancy to such a trifling object, and he was ashamed in front of his wife. Velga was particularly attentive and considerate these days; she always found something to say when she entered or left the room or when she came across her husband in the yard. True, she did not speak of important matters, but rather of the usual details of everyday life and the work that had to be done; but she wanted to consult her husband about everything. When she went to the cowshed or to the cellar, she wore a red carnation in her hair. It seemed childish, but perhaps it was no more so than his keeping Annina's toy on the table.

One day the wooden pear had again been hidden away, this time in the cupboard. Edvarts did not ask any questions; he searched patiently until he found it, and put it back in its former place. Later, he passed the window and, happening to raise his eyes, caught sight of his wife looking at the toy. He was startled to see her face contorted with hatred and anguish. She noticed him, and quickly turned away. But she never dared touch the toy again.

This battle had been fought out in silence, but it was as though a wedge had been driven between them. Henceforth there were four people living in the house: two who met every day, exchanged indifferent or polite words, and lived like man and wife — and two who kept silent, watched each other furtively, suddenly started up when the other had fallen asleep, and searched the sleeper's face with silent, mortified questioning.

Edvarts thought his wife was to blame for this double life. Why had she not simply taken the toy from the table in his presence, saying, "I don't like it"? Instead she had removed it secretly, perhaps thinking that he would forget all about it; or maybe she had wanted to put something to the test. But what? Perhaps he himself was a little to blame. When Annina was still quite small, he remembered, his wife had often called on her cousin and had been affectionate toward the little girl; she had behaved as women usually behave with other people's children. His own fondness for the little girl had gone on increasing, while his wife's attitude toward Annina had changed.

Now that he carefully considered all these things it suddenly struck him with full force that Velga had never felt for Annina as one feels for a child; there had always been something strange, something like secret jealousy. He had probably been wrong to act as he did. Of course, Velga was unhappy because she had no children of her own. And her husband had neglected her because of a child that belonged to other people. The toy reminded her of it all. That was why she hated it, why she suffered. Dishes slipped from her fingers, her feet stumbled on level ground, at night she tossed about as though in a fever, she talked wildly in her sleep. They were disconnected words, they made no sense. Sometimes they sounded like a garbled prayer. She often went to church these days. Even at the funeral she had been the last to leave; she had prayed with tears in her eyes, and cried even more than the mother herself.

Something had to be done to restore peace to them both. One night, when Velga was again tossing about in the grip of a nightmare, Edvarts wakened her.

"You talk in your sleep, Velga, almost every night. What is the matter?"

She started up into a sitting position and looked at him with the bewildered eyes of a hunted thing. "I don't talk, no, it isn't true!"

"What is frightening you, Velga dearest? . . . Come, let's talk it over, for once."

"Yes . . . talk about what?" Now she sat there quietly and regarded her husband with a sad, searching look. Edvarts suddenly felt sorry for her. Oh God! So many years had passed since they had got married like two people possessed, crazy with love for each other as if a spell had been cast over them, and she was still the same beautiful Velga she had been then. But something was over and done with.

Perhaps Edvarts only felt sorry thinking of the past, of the days when there had been everything, but which were of no help now. No, he would pull himself together. They were both young, they had not lived half their lives yet. There was still so much for him to take up and to complete. Now he was going to gladden his wife's heart. He began to tell her about all the things that were still unfinished or had so far not even been considered. About the new orchard and the arbor, about the cattle and about wine-making, about the prospects opening up to farming when the laying of the new narrow-gauge railroad was completed in their neighborhood, about the motor-bicycle he had long been anxious to buy and which he had actually looked over at a shop in Riga. His wife listened and cried. Well, he thought, that's as it should be — women always cry, when they're happy and when they're unhappy.

"And as to Annina's toy, let's put it away together this time, you and I. There's no sense in it anyway. Why don't you tell me quite plainly that you don't like me to keep it on the table?" His own frankness and goodwill warmed his heart; he smiled. Velga burst into a torrent of tears and clung to her husband's shoulder, her fingers convulsively digging into his flesh and hurting him.

"Now, now, have a good cry, it will pass, everything passes," Edvarts whispered, stroking Velga's black curls. Strange: it was so long since he had stroked her hair. Yet this was the same girl who had once given him sleepless nights. Now she was clinging to his shoulder, and she was sobbing. It looked like a fit of hysteria.

He freed himself from her grasp and went to fetch a glass of cold tea from the kitchen. When he returned his wife was sitting on the edge of the bed, her light wrap about her; she was quiet and silent, her vacant eyes stared at the table. There stood Annina's toy. Velga gulped down the tea. Edvarts put the glass on the table, smiled, and reached for the toy, intending to put it into the drawer. But his movement was too sudden; his fingers knocked against the toy, and it fell to the floor and rolled toward the bed. With a terrible scream Velga staggered to her feet and stood, panting, at the head of the bed.

"Merciful heavens! What's the matter with you? Have you gone mad?"

He picked up the toy and slowly, deliberately put it away in the drawer; he stood still for a while as if turning something over in his mind, and when he looked round at his wife his face was blank and expressionless. Velga's eyes opened unnaturally wide, in all their blackness, full of terror.

"Where were you when Annina was drowned?" asked Edvarts, his voice dry and toneless.

"I was in Kalns's shop; I bought herrings and washing soda," Velga answered quickly, as if in a hurry.

"How do you know it happened just *then*?"

"No, I don't know, I didn't go anywhere else, I thought it happened just at that time."

With a few long strides Edvarts crossed the room and caught hold of his wife's hair; her head knocked against the wall.

"How did it happen? You led her to the jetty and pushed her in?"

"No — no — Edvarts — it wasn't like that. . . . She was by the edge of the lake . . . I happened to pass — from the shop. . . . She herself wanted . . ."

"What did she want?"

"Waterlilies — I also wanted —"

"And she fell in by *herself*?" Edvarts's hand tightened its grip on his wife's hair. "Tell me the truth, *now* at least tell me the truth! You didn't push her?"

"Only a bit, Edvarts, a very little bit . . . I don't know how it happened, I didn't think she'd fall — we wanted to step into the boat."

"And you didn't do anything to save her? You ran away?"

Velga did not answer. Unblinking, her wide-open eyes stared into her husband's face. Edvarts raised the other hand as if to strike her, but he suddenly felt very tired; he let go of her hair and sat down on the chair, dully contemplating the palm of his hand and some black hairs that had got caught between his fingers.

"Tell me at least that you were frightened, that you didn't know what to do," he slowly began after a while.

"I was frightened, I didn't know what to do," Velga repeated hurriedly, like a lesson learned by heart.

"And you did not scream, you did not call for help? You had a guilty conscience —"

She made no answer.

"Nobody saw you?"

"No."

"But that makes no difference . . . that makes no difference at all . . . " He rocked his head in his hands, mechanically, like one of those clockwork mandarins that keep nodding their heads, and his foot beat time on the floor. Then his movements slowed down; he froze into immobility, feeling nothing, thinking nothing. As if from far away he heard that his wife was dressing, that she went to the door, opened it, and stood there. She stood there for a long time.

"Edvarts . . ." she called, once, twice, and her voice became lower and lower.

But Edvarts did not answer. He did not grasp anything, did not understand anything, least of all this fiendish, self-devouring love of hers.

Velga went. The door closed slowly, noiselessly.

The next day she was found in the lake. Not far from the spot where Annina had drowned.

THE LEAVETAKING

THE regiment was retreating, but the company had to advance in order to protect a crossroads of which the village was more or less the center. Really, the village was only a cluster of small houses in the southeastern quadrant, with a brook on its south side. The roads divided outside the village — on the northern hill. A few enemy tanks had clattered down the south road in pursuit of the retreating regiment. This road was mined. But with a view to deceiving the enemy into a feeling of self-confidence, the bridge across the brook had not been blown up.

Captain Straume's company was moving north and, in the shelter of the brush along the brook, was approaching the village. The captain had chosen the moment when the last rays of the setting sun were level with the roof tops, and the enemy, no longer expecting a counter-attack, had begun to portion out supper. He even allowed the enemy to finish the meal, knowing that after a meal the human mind is apt to become sluggish and careless. Besides, the setting sun — so the captain figured — was dazzling the eyes of the enemy's outposts in the east.

After careful scrutiny it appeared that the village had been occupied only by a scouting patrol which had followed the tanks. A few minutes before dusk fell, the company rapidly advanced upon the village — without giving the enemy machine gunners a chance to recover from their surprise and to take aim at the human forms that came tumbling across the open meadow.

Hand grenades silenced the two machine guns on the edge of the village — as well as the lieutenant in charge of the patrol, who had run out into the main street, still munching something and vainly trying to fasten his belt in the right hole. The captain observed this calamity with an expert eye: the belt is the coordinator of mind and feet and the maintainer of discipline if something goes wrong — but thinking is not disciplined; it gets entangled in trifles and leads the thinker to perdition.

The soldiers searched the houses, directing those of the enemy who were willing to surrender, and throwing a hand grenade or two through the window or door of the huts if nobody responded and the silence seemed suspicious. None of the inhabitants were left in the village. The captain interrogated a dozen scared and half-witted prisoners, only to learn what he had already surmised: heavier tanks, artillery, and infantry would arrive the next day, in such numbers as to make him unwilling to meet them. His victory was but a small dent in the enemy's armor, a victory which could change nothing in the course of the war, which could only make it easier for his regiment to retreat. And this, indeed, was Captain Straume's task in the battle of the withdrawal.

He now ordered the bridge across the brook blown up, in case some of the enemy tanks should wish to return, and posted several sentries with anti-tank guns. He knew that the enemy leaders were more methodical than shrewd and that they did not trouble about the lives of their soldiers. But Straume had to be concerned about every single one of his: he did not want to have wounded men. In addition, he had to calculate as if every cartridge were a precious stone; he was forced to dole them out with utmost economy, knowing that an abundance of ammunition encourages soldiers to aim inaccurately as a means of overcoming their feelings of defeat.

92

Tomorrow all hell would let loose in the village. The company had to retreat before dawn. It was midsummer, and the sun would rise early, casting its light on nothing but misery and hatred in a company that had long since ceased to be a company — there were only three platoons which, for that matter, were no longer platoons either: only a total of eighty-four men.

Lieutenant Kamis entered to report that there had been no losses and that all men had been quartered; he remained standing for a while, smoking, waiting for orders. An orderly brought in coffee, and the captain asked him to fetch another cup for the lieutenant. Kamis had been snatched from his last term at the Technical College and had not started shaving until he was in the army. The captain liked the boy, who kept himself aloof — always remaining, as it were, behind an invisible screen.

"Are we retreating?" asked the lieutenant.

The captain gave a short, dry laugh. "We are advancing, lieutenant! In a linear dimension we are retreating, in another way we are going forward. For instance, you are much older and manlier than you were half a year ago, aren't you? *You* are advancing!"

There was something behind the captain's speech, and the lieutenant decided to stick to the official tone, although the cup of coffee and the chair pushed toward him by the captain seemed to invite candor.

"I'm obeying your orders, sir."

"You have to, otherwise you wouldn't be alive, damn it. . . . You ran a trifle too fast, and if they on the other side hadn't been so lazy I shouldn't have the pleasure of talking to you."

"Yes, sir, but we are retreating, aren't we?"

"You might not even know that, for if you fall your nose will be pointing ahead."

"It will, captain, unless at that very moment I should be happening to look back at you, sir."

Captain Straume laughed. They both laughed.

Encouraged by the laughter, the lieutenant said, "We are going to trample on our own people soon; the face of the war is changing. Although we have become involved in it against our will, we have been advancing, hoping to crush the enemy. Then we stopped, assuming that he would collapse. And now we believe that he will get exhausted pursuing us." The lieutenant blushed, thinking he had said too much; he had to do it, however, sooner or later.

The captain smiled. "A child playing or building with his toys gets fed up with even the nicest ones before long; he will knock them over, leave them scattered on the floor, and start on something new. That doesn't directly apply to us — the small nations — although we are no better. This game is played by bigger children, and we are involved in it; do you want leave, lieutenant?"

Kamis flushed. "I haven't asked for it."

"I know. Nor can you get it before we are out of this hole. But your mother would love to see you."

Kamis was reflecting.

"There are a great many mothers. You've never been on leave, captain?"

"That isn't of such great importance as you might like to think at this moment. I have nowhere to go. You may sympathize and shrug your shoulders. Why? I haven't been deceived by anything. As you were saying, the face of the war is changing. We advance, obeying orders, and, slightly dazed, we come to a stop and think: How nice it would be to be at home!

"Finally we retreat, with the knowledge of the value of human life — of the Johns and Peters in our company who haven't been brought up to shoot and hate people. Yet in the same fashion, we would some day stand beside the graves of our relatives, with bowed heads; and you would experience just the same pangs as now, tormenting yourself with jealousy at some girl's threshold, and sleep less comfortably than you do at the front. All afflictions have been suffered before and will be again in future. War is terrible not because of the quality but because of the quantity of its events. War is an intensified process of life, with greater hatred, greater love. Or do you think we could enter the heavenly realms as we are? I wouldn't know what to do there."

"You might get the command of a regiment there," the lieutenant suggested timidly.

The captain almost choked, gulping down a mouthful of coffee, and looked at the lieutenant with a face expanded in a broad smile such as few of the men ever had the chance to see.

"Do you want me to become a band master? But I know what you mean, or else I wouldn't be your superior."

Kamis bent his head and clicked his heels under the chair.

The captain winked his left eye, as was his habit. "You must not do that, and you damned well know that you mustn't, for it would mean trifling with military discipline, for which I haven't given any occasion."

"I beg your pardon, captain."

"You want to know what the sense of war is; some sense can always be invented. If a species has multiplied too rapidly, nature will intervene with epidemics against which medicine will fight, or with ideas for which we ourselves will be killed."

"That's rational, but our sufferings are irrational," Kamis remarked.

"That might be the purpose of this process. For otherwise you would only stand up for the idea of good food and a comfortable bed for yourself, or, at best, you'd wish others to have the same."

"You don't believe that yourself?"

The captain winked his left eye and continued. "But even in that process there is a difference between how an army and a nation will go to meet destruction — in an irrational way, as you said. In the present war you probably wouldn't cross the street to save Hitler, Churchill, or Stalin; but you learn your duty and begin to love it in such a way that as soon as John or Peter is in danger you will unhesitatingly stake your life to save him! Or wouldn't you? I imagine that was all you wanted to know. Well, then, you'll start moving with the second and third platoons at two o'clock in the morning. None of the Great Powers has had the least scruple about exploiting our work and making us sacrifice our lives. It is up to us to know how to preserve these things. At two o'clock, then; good-night, lieutenant."

The captain drank the remainder of his coffee, unbuttoned the collar of his tunic, put his flashlight and revolver within easy reach, passed his hand over his tired eyes, and prepared to lie down to sleep deeply and exactly as long as time permitted. He was fortunate enough to be able to fall asleep even between two gunshots, as his men would laughingly say, but once he woke up he did so in a moment — completely, and without yawning.

Then too, he no longer experienced a moment of extreme anguish just before his own company's or the enemy's attack: the first silent moment when — though a single shot has not been fired — every man's fate hangs in the balance, as it were, and each man is more profoundly frightened than he is later in the din of battle — which he can get used to in fifteen minutes. Of course he still knew moments of terror; he had learned to let his mind and will respond immediately. Any unexpected noise — the dropping of a fork, the flutter of a night moth behind the windowblind, or the honking of a motorcar — instead of startling him would find him with clenched fists. On the other hand, whenever he was supposed to give an address, to talk to his superiors, to be at a party where he might get acquainted with pleasant likeable people, his mouth would turn dry, his hands clammy with perspiration — and then when some trifling incident aroused him he was able to express himself vigorously. The war's many wrath-provoking situations had engrossed him. In fact, the commander of the regiment had given the captain the task of covering the retreat because he was aware of this ability to perform well when angry.

In the farmhouse which was to accommodate the captain for the night there were a bed, a table, and a couple of benches. In the center of one wall was a plain door made of planks, possibly leading to a larder or to the loft. It could be bolted from inside by means of a wooden bar. The bar was pushed across, locking the door.

Before going to bed the captain walked about the room, minutely examining it. From behind the door he heard a sound, as if someone were panting or groaning. He unbolted the door, and, with a sudden movement, swung it open and stepped behind it — even wounded men would occasionally fire, and mines were sometimes fastened to the legs of cats and dogs; he had learned to be cautious. Framed in the doorway appeared the face of a boy nine or ten, with eyes wide open, fair curly hair that hung down on his forehead, and hands that were raised as if in prayer. His lips were murmuring incoherent words: "House . . . fire . . . gate . . . milk . . ." was all the captain could make out.

"We still have the house, my boy," the captain said, "where is your mother?"

The boy evidently did not understand the question and continued to mutter something and to stretch out his folded hands toward the captain. He patted the boy's head, lifted the eyelids with his thumb, and knew by the expression of the eyes that the boy was mentally deranged. But it was such an extremely beautiful face, with fine, delicate features. The lock of hair falling down on his forehead added to it an expression of sadness, as if this creature were chosen to express some beautiful thought or dream. The captain shouted for the orderly in the adjoining room, raising his voice more than was usual for him, thinking the man would be asleep. But the orderly evidently was not, for he was there in no time, like a shot. Nor did he look surprised, only slightly apprehensive.

"Get something for the boy to eat; look in my bag."

"I gave him some food already, sir! He fell asleep in the loft. I thought he wouldn't disturb you."

97

"You should have reported him! I cannot possibly search every nook and cranny. The devil knows who may hide here. Understand?"

"Yes, sir, I understand."

"Take the boy away!"

"Where to, sir?"

The captain cast a piercing look at the orderly's face with its slightly contracted eyebrows, although the rest of it showed the usual expression of subordination to military discipline.

The captain waved his hand, and the orderly stood at ease.

"Got some blankets? The loft will be cold in the morning."

"There are no blankets, sir, not any more. I'd better take him back to the loft where he came from."

Once more the captain passed his hand over his tired eyes, after glancing over the bare room where there was no piece of furniture suitable for resting on, except his own bed.

"All right. Turn in, go!" The captain placed the boy on the side of the bed nearest the wall, covered him, and soothed him. He held his breath for a moment when the boy's arms clasped his neck; and then the child fell asleep.

The captain had known that the only freedom fate still granted him was to choose whether to sleep on his left or his right side. But now he had not even this choice left, for he was afraid he might wake the boy. He himself could not fall asleep. "If only I had a son like him, as beautiful as he is!" he was thinking. "But then it's the beauty of madness, that's why he is here, abandoned by his parents and all. . . . Or is it the beauty of panic, which might be cured?"

The captain was awakened by a dull detonation close to the wall of the house.

"Mine throwers!" he muttered, reaching for his torch, watch, and pistol. "Starting early." In half a minute he was up and dressed, ready for the fighting that was his task in life. Another explosion resounded to the south of the house.

The captain took a step toward the door, then stopped short as if held back by something, flashed the beam of his torch over the boy who did not wake but continued to sleep with rosy lips, tousled hair, and arms extended to where the captain had been lying.

"Oh God, I can't help it, I can't, really, I must be going!" he said, losing a few seconds on this reflection. Seconds that were fatal. The third charge of the mine thrower caught the captain as he was stepping over the threshold.

 **ONE-DAY LAND**

VALDIS was half man, half legend — perhaps even more legend than man; for, in addition to what others had to tell about him, which was incredible enough, there were also his own tales about himself, and they were more incredible still. He regarded the world as his own private dream, likely to be invaded at any moment by a meddlesome nightmarish apparition — his wife. She was a small, round, energetic woman endowed with a wonderful gift for tracking down her husband, no matter which saloon in the suburbs he was hiding in. Actually, there was no great necessity for his presence at home. She owned a little house on the outskirts of the town, an orchard, and a vegetable garden; there her husband did some pruning and hoeing. The management of the place was entirely in the wife's hands; he received a small amount of pocket money, for pipe tobacco and tram fares, and that was all he had.

But there was always someone willing to stand him a pint of beer, and he repaid it by telling his strange stories. In proportion to the strength and quantity of the drinks he was given, his mind embarked on extravagant fantasies; sometimes, carried away by his own yarn, even he himself seemed no longer able to distinguish between fact and fiction. For this reason, nothing very definite was known about his past. According to his own version, he had been a sailor in his

100

young days; then he had studied something or other; later on, he had traded in something or other and had gone bankrupt; finally, opining that a man must experience absolutely everything in order to become a real man, he had taken a wife — or had been taken as a husband.

He had thick black hair and a cleanshaven, sunburnt face which gave no clue to his age; always neat and tidy, his clothes cut like a sailor's, he went the round of the small taverns, puffing at his pipe and recounting his strange adventures. In his own words, he was like a ship withdrawn from service but still fulfilling a nautical purpose — like a clubhouse for yachtsmen which is no longer the prey of tempests but instead the scene of many a dance and drinking bout.

He was said to be an exceptionally gifted man; and it was not surprising that his wife had married him, hoping to make a useful citizen out of him. He had disappointed her hopes and, as he laughingly said, it served her right: if he had seriously intended to become a great man he would have never married a woman like her. As things were, they suited each other perfectly, and there was no cause for discontent on either side. Indeed, he had some good qualities, but in his wife's opinion they merely helped, in some strange way, to promote entirely unpleasant traits: perseverance — his bent for slipping away from home, patience — his ability to wait for someone to stand him a drink, a love of truth — his quick detection of other people's faults, steadfastness — his predilection for drink, and ingenuity — his knack for inventing idle nonsense.

Therefore, notwithstanding these noble qualities, he was said to have been unable to apply himself to any kind of work for long. As a student, he seemed to have tried his hand at poetry. Unable to arrive at a style of his own, he had turned to imitating the verse of others — so successfully, indeed, that he started to send his poems, signed with the names of other poets, to various publishers. Some poems were so good that they were actually published, and the poets under whose names they appeared hesitated to disown them.

101

The whole thing came to light when one day, finding himself in serious financial difficulties, he had tried to obtain payment for a poem by using another poet's name. Later he worked in the harbor master's office but was dismissed because he had made a certain remark which, in his own opinion, was perfectly innocent: when his superior at the office was promoted he had merely said: "The higher an ape climbs up a tree the more visible it becomes that he is an ape!"

Well, now you have seen what kind of person Valdis was! Such a man's stories have to be taken with a grain of salt; of course, one cannot believe everything one hears. Therefore I shall relate only the most credible of his tales, roughly in the way he told it himself.

+ + +

That autumn, I was still a student. I had rather neglected a few subjects since the spring, and now I had to pull myself together and make up for lost time. I was just looking for new lodgings, some quiet little room in which I could devote myself to serious study, when I ran into an old friend of mine, a clerk. He said, "It is difficult to concentrate on studies when one lives in Riga. All sorts of things may distract you even while you are wandering about, looking for a room. You are welcome to my cottage at the seaside. I've just moved out, but my lease doesn't expire until the middle of October. There you would have all the peace and quiet you can possibly wish for. If you like the idea — here's the key!"

I made a note of the address, and the following day I left for the seaside — which, incidentally, is more beautiful than ever when there is no longer any one there to admire it.

The clear, untroubled calm of late summer enveloped the gardens, in which asters and dahlias bloomed in unearthly beauty. There was hardly anyone to be seen in the streets; if one walked with a firm tread, one's footsteps reverberated dully, as they do in an empty room; and involuntarily one trod more softly, loath to disturb the radiant stillness that reigned everywhere. Occasionally, a bird abruptly struck up its little song — sparkling, golden notes among the foliage of maples and lime trees gently touched with the yellow and purple tints of autumn.

Yes, it was a beautiful morning when I arrived at the seaside and looked for the bungalow to which my friend had given me the key. After a while I found it, tucked away behind a luxurious summer villa. It was surrounded by lilac bushes which had run wild and grown a tangled mass of branches; its dark, overshadowed windows seemed to regard me with an air of mystery. A spider web, silvery with dew, hung suspended across the doorknob; a frightened spider quickly lowered itself from it, and I had to destroy the web as I opened the door. That's how it is, I thought, the one has his house pulled down so that the other can take up his abode.

There were only two rooms and a kitchen. I unpacked my few belongings, opened all the doors and windows, sat down on the bed, and felt strangely agitated. The silence was so great that I found it difficult to get accustomed to it. My arms and legs seemed to have lost their power of movement, and my brain refused to produce a single coherent thought.

I spent the day wandering about by the seashore. In the evening it took me a long time to fall asleep, and I kept looking at the green wallpaper and the solitary picture that adorned the room. It hung facing me, at the foot of my bed; it was an unframed, rather crumpled print, fastened to the wall with a pin. Very likely it wasn't my friend's property; by the look of it, it must have beguiled the eyes of generations of tenants. It represented a young lady leaning over a balustrade, dressed in something like a Greek tunic. The picture was certainly no work of art, but one could raise no objections to the young lady herself. If it had been a photograph, any man would have tried to find out something about the original: who she was, what her circumstances were, and where one might meet her. But since it was a print, such efforts would have been fruitless.

Yet the young lady occupied my mind — not only on that first

103

evening but on all the following mornings and evenings whenever, tired out with concentrated study, I rested my eyes on the picture. I even smoothed it out and fastened it more securely to the wall with two additional pins. After all, the picture was the only thing there was to look at.

With me, no kind of work has ever presented any great difficulties in itself, but I always find it hard to settle down to it. The moment I try to make a start there seem to be far more interesting things to do than the work at hand or the things I ought to be doing. My friend had been right in suggesting the seaside because it would offer me no escape from my studies. All the same, he did not really know me! The more I crammed my head full of learning in the evenings the harder it was to make it work again in the mornings. Sometimes I was in despair. The only distraction I had was the young lady at the foot of my bed.

I began to stay in bed half an hour longer in the morning to contemplate her and to have an excuse for postponing the moment when I'd have to sit over my books again. I suppose there is nothing new in such a situation. It often happens that the pages of a book lose all their attraction when a young man begins to study the beauty of a girl's face. With me it was slightly different: I went on working, but the greyness of my studies increased my liking for the young lady. She was the only thing I could turn to in my loneliness. And that is why I fell madly in love with her. I even composed a poem in her honor:

> Oh, you're the only one who understands
> That I don't care for learning and for books;
> Forgiving me my unwashed face and hands,
> You smile upon me and my amorous looks.

One day I decided to give her a name. I thought of many, but could not make up my mind. Finally I resorted to my pocket diary, in which there was a name opposite each day of the year; I thrust my finger haphazardly between the pages and, well, there it was, just where I was pointing, in black and white: Iza! Now that she had a name I could begin to converse with her. True enough, she made me no answer, but that's no great matter. When a young man speaks of his feelings to a girl she usually doesn't say very much — not until he finally proposes to her. Really it is only after the wedding that she really gets into her stride, and then the husband is amazed at the commonplace language that issues from such beautiful lips!

The thirteenth of September was Iza's name-day. I shall never forget it. . . . I decided to celebrate and have a holiday, and it gave me great satisfaction to pack away my books. I decorated the room with beautiful autumn flowers and bought myself a bottle of strong liquor. It was a Saturday, and I was late with my shopping. Besides, the tavern around the corner no longer stocked good brands of spirits, now that the summer visitors had left. This was the last remaining bottle on the shelf; one could see from the label that it was an odd kind of drink — so odd, indeed, that there had been no demand for it. The landlord smiled when he realized he did not remember its price. We examined the bottle but could not make out the language on the label. Finally, by mutual agreement, we decided upon a price.

That evening, a wind arose, blowing from the sea. The pine trees groaned as their branches swayed in the wind, and single drops of rain occasionally beat against the window. I lit a fire in the little iron stove, prepared my dinner and drank the first glass to Iza's health. I don't know what mysterious concoction it was, and I can't remember what exactly happened, but I woke up in a town I had never seen before.

Judging by the sun, which shone almost directly overhead, it was about noon. As far as the eye could see, large beautiful buildings of white stone rose to majestic heights beside the promenade which seemed also to be the main thoroughfare of the town. Outlined against the calm blue sea, exotic trees rustled and swayed in a light breeze. Friendly, smiling people walked past me. I had been dozing on a bench in the shade, and nobody paid any attention to me. My surprise was all the greater, therefore, when a little boy came up to me and announced: "Miss Iza is waiting for you!" I gave him a coin and asked where I could find her. He pointed to a house in the distance, and I immediately recognized it, probably by the balustrades. Without wasting another moment, I set out toward it; but then all sorts of things happened, and my progress was delayed.

With drums beating and a brass band playing regimental marches, a column of soldiers emerged from a side street. It was headed by a stately colonel on horseback who now and then smiled and waved to the cheering crowd. As often happens, great numbers of idle people accompanied the soldiers, and there were pretty girls who threw them flowers and shouted encouraging words about victory and a happy homecoming. From this I concluded that the war had only just begun.

The sight of something unusual always fills me with joy, and this time my elation was increased by the thought that I wouldn't have to bother about examinations after all. The only thing that marred my happiness was the fear that a mobilization order might be waiting for me at home. Besides, the weapons the soldiers carried were not of the kind I had been taught to use when I was doing my military service. It did not look like a modern army, and I thought that a few machineguns could easily put it to flight. Then I noticed a young lieutenant sitting on the terrace of a café close by; I went across and joined him, hoping that he would explain a few things to me. We drank coffee. It was not difficult to begin a conversation for he was a talkative man and full of confidence.

"Tomorrow we shall win a great victory," he said. "It is absolutely certain; right is on our side!"

I could not shake his faith by arguing that right alone was not enough, and that the army instructors seemed to have fallen somewhat behind in the art of warfare. After a while I left the lieutenant and continued on my way. At the next corner I met a kindly old woman who was selling roses. I asked her to make up a beautiful bouquet for me, but when it came to paying she refused my money.

"Is this a particularly happy day for you, too?" I asked, thanking her.

"Yes, today I give my flowers away for nothing! Tomorrow my son is coming out of prison, and I won't sell flowers tomorrow."

The police obviously had also to be reckoned with in this place — I wondered uneasily whether my papers were in order.

The old woman wanted to tell me something more about her son, but a young man came up to her and, like me, demanded a large bunch of roses; he did not seem in the least surprised, though, when he got them for nothing.

"This is a great day for me. My new book of poems has come out!" He waved it under my nose; it was a slender volume, entitled *One-Day Land*. I had a look at the poems, and they did not strike me as particularly good. I asked whether there had already been a review of the book.

"Not yet — tomorrow, perhaps. But the reviews are bound to be good. The critics can't possibly fail to realize that I'm a genius!" the young man replied, smiling.

I did not want to disillusion him. Let him enjoy his happiness today, I thought; tomorrow will come soon enough and shatter his hopes. Therefore I said nothing and took my leave.

Just then I caught sight of a man selling newspapers. I hastily picked up the latest edition of the *One-Day News*, hoping that now at last I'd gain some information about this strange town. The leading article extolled the country's new constitution; another article announced an increase in workers' wages, to come into force tomorrow. Not a word about the war anywhere! The editors must be a sleepy lot, I thought. I decided to delay no longer but go straight to the house where I was expected.

There was Iza, leaning over the balustrade, exactly as I had imagined: her dainty skin all soft and rosy, her brown hair sparkling with light, and, encircled by magnificent lashes, her starry eyes like deep blue violets . . .

"At last you have come!" she said. "I have been waiting for you so long!" And she offered me her full, cherry-red lips . . .

+   +   +

"Well, you do have rather wonderful dreams!" I interrupted, unable to contain myself any longer.

Valdis gave a start and looked at me with a surprised, indignant air. "That was no dream!" he said tersely and put his glass of beer to his mouth with such relish that it seemed he was still savoring Iza's first kiss.

Trying to look unconcerned, I hummed a little tune and drank some beer. At last he went on with his story.

+   +   +

Naturally, I was rather surprised to get such a warm welcome, and I explained that I hadn't visited her sooner because I'd been busy working for my examinations.

"Oh, your examinations. . . . You'll pass them all tomorrow. Believe me!" She said it with such conviction that I began to think she was right.

Iza chatted about many things; she thanked me for the flowers and added that she could not have imagined a more delightful beginning to her name-day.

"Excuse me," I blurted out, "it seems to me that your name-day was yesterday."

"Yesterday," she repeated thoughtfully, and then she gave a quick laugh as though she hadn't quite understood me but did not think it very important. "Yes, today is my name-day. But tomorrow, after you have passed your examinations, we'll celebrate our engagement and invite all our friends. Won't we?" She lovingly put her arm round my shoulders.

108

I tried not to show my astonishment. We went into the drawing room where a richly laid table greeted my eyes. I looked around to see if her parents or some other relatives weren't perhaps hiding somewhere, but I did not notice anything suspicious. When I asked her she said briefly that she was living by herself. Having only just met her, I did not think it right to ask questions about her family and her material circumstances; so I said nothing, ate the cake she offered me, and left all the talking to her. I hoped I might indirectly glean something from her words that would reassure me — after all, I was only a poor student and could not hope to maintain a family. Besides, she was evidently accustomed to wealth and comfort. But no enlightenment came to me; on the contrary, there only came one wine after the other and, as I drank, my doubts and fears gradually faded away. I heard a harp being played somewhere in the distance; the promenade was aflame with the glorious colors of sunset; we wined and dined, and we kissed . . . and then — I can't quite remember what happened then. I woke up . . .

+ + +

"In bed?" I again interrupted him.

"No!" Valdis retorted sharply. "On the bench by the sea, and this time it was the brass band that woke me. The wine had given me a thick head and a buzzing in my ears, and therefore I couldn't immediately recollect the events of the previous day. But the column of soldiers passing by seemed vaguely familiar. They made a brave show as they marched away along the promenade; girls threw them flowers and shouted about victory and a happy homecoming. My friend of the previous day, the lieutenant, was again drinking coffee on the terrace of the café. I went up to him, said Good morning, and sat down beside him."

+ + +

"Has your detachment not yet departed for the front?" I began the conversation.

109

"No, we are leaving today, toward evening."

"But will there be anything left for you to do?" I joked somewhat maliciously. "You foretold a great victory for today, you know!"

"No, for tomorrow. Tomorrow we shall win a great victory. It is absolutely certain; right is on our side!"

"Now, look here," I said angrily, "that's exactly what you told me yesterday!"

"Yesterday?" he repeated, baffled. "No, the war started today."

He struck me as a man of very limited intelligence, and it was quite obvious that he was excessively influenced by his country's propaganda. I left him and went to look for Iza's house. On my way there, I tried to remember what had happened the night before. I had the uneasy feeling that she had thrown me out. Perhaps I had said something rude or had behaved so objectionably that she would never forgive me? I was overjoyed when I caught sight of the old woman selling roses: perhaps flowers would help me to win back Iza's favor, if I presented them to her with expressions of deepest remorse and contrition.

I asked the old woman to make up an even larger bouquet than on the day before. Again she refused to accept my money. "Today I give my flowers away for nothing! Tomorrow my son is coming out of prison, and I won't sell flowers tomorrow."

"But that's what you told me yesterday!" I protested.

She was as puzzled as the lieutenant had been. "No — yesterday . . . yesterday there wasn't anything . . ." She tried hard to recall some long forgotten idea, but she had to give up, and continued in her former joyful mood: "Tomorrow, tomorrow he'll be free . . ."

At that moment the young man approached with his book of poems, looking just as happy as before. He was very friendly and obliging, and told me everything I wanted to know about the book. All the poems in the volume had been conceived in one single day, in one glorious moment of inspiration. There had been no withering blast from the critics yet.

110

There's something very odd going on here, I thought, and I hurried away to buy the *One-Day News*. It was yesterday's edition. These people are the most backward lot on earth, I thought, curse them all! Then I noticed that there was no date on the paper, and my uneasiness increased.

As I approached Iza's house I saw her already from a long way off — there she was, smiling and leaning over the balustrade. She received me with a kiss and was as affectionate as before. Thank God! There can't have been any unpleasantness yesterday after all, I concluded. This made me so happy, and my brain was still so affected by my hangover, that I asked no questions. I sat down at the table which was laid as before. Soon I was thoroughly enjoying myself. Our conversation flowed on so merrily while the harp was playing that I forgot my resolution to drink rather less and instead keep an eye on what was going on around me. Gradually I began to feel sleepy.

"Listen, darling," I said at last, "do you remember what happened yesterday?"

"Yesterday?" she frowned. "What is the meaning of yesterday? I don't know such a word."

"Today will be yesterday when we meet again tomorrow."

She laughed. "Oh, my dearest, you're telling me something I can't possibly understand. I'm only a woman . . ." and she kissed me again. I felt slightly dizzy . . . And then I awoke on the bench by the sea!

+   +   +

"Look here, my dear sir!" I cried indignantly. "Do you expect me to believe this? It makes no sense at all!"

+   +   +

That's what I thought, too. And that's why I decided to be more careful on the following day. I intended to have a good look at the town and explore other parts of it as well. But some powerful magic

111

seemed to draw me to Iza's house. I was madly in love. Besides, my hangover wasn't getting any better.

This time I drank only a few glasses of wine and emptied the others into the flower pots when Iza wasn't looking. Toward evening I was again overcome by such drowsiness that I could barely keep my eyes open. But I turned away when Iza embraced me and tried to kiss me once more. She fell asleep in my arms. I laid her down on the blue silk divan.

At that same moment the lights began to go out everywhere in the town, and all the noises died down. I could still hear the music of the harp, but it gradually receded until it faded away altogether. Luckily, I had my flashlight with me, and I decided to have a closer look at the house. There wasn't anything there! There was nothing but empty space, and those many doors were an absolute swindle — they did not open on to anything, they led nowhere. It was as though I were amid the scenery on a stage, with the difference that I could not make my way behind the scenes.

Finally I discovered a narrow flight of steps which seemed to lead to a cellar. I descended into a long passage and groped my way toward a faint glimmer of light at its far end. At last I came to a large hall which looked like a gigantic study, crammed full of books, charts, diagrams, and all sorts of weird instruments. These things so absorbed my attention that at first I didn't notice the queer little old man who stood beside me and who must have been watching me for quite a while. I gave a start when I caught sight of him, but he himself did not seem particularly surprised at this meeting. He sternly beckoned me to follow him and led me to a recess opening off the hall. It was pleasantly furnished: there were soft chairs, and a vase of flowers stood on the table. This was probably where he rested from his labors. He opened a small wall cupboard and produced a bottle of wine and a glass.

"No, no!" I shouted. "I know that wine! Drink it yourself!"

The old man seemed rather annoyed, but he did not drink any of the wine. He made me sit down on the chair opposite him and asked angrily:

"What are you doing here?"

"I? Nothing in particular — just on a visit, as it were."

"You should have gone to bed long ago!"

"Is there a specific hour at which everyone in this place has to go to bed?" I retorted.

The old man sadly shook his head. "I was right when I thought you'd give me trouble. You've already managed to confuse some people's minds in this town, and now — now you don't even want to sleep but go gallivanting about!"

"Listen," I said, "you seem to be the most intelligent person in this town. Would you please explain what's going on here?"

"Don't you like it here?" he countered my question.

"I can't say that I don't like it. But everything is at a standstill in this place; nothing gets anywhere, neither that smart looking lot of soldiers nor my engagement."

The old man looked at me thoughtfully.

"Why should you want to get anything moving? Would it be better if our soldiers came back wounded and defeated? This is One-Day Land. Here everyone re-lives the happiest day of his life and gives himself up to his fondest hopes . . ."

"Which never come true," I interposed.

"They would not come true in any case; even if they did, their fulfillment would never come up to people's expectations. All the people who live here have at some time been disappointed in their hopes. Man is ruled by Time. All his life he tries to seize hold of something that will not slip away and vanish together with him. Yet, when all is said and done, his acquisitions are like objects on a ship — they can be touched and held, but they float with the ship on the waves, and sooner or later they are swallowed up by the sea. Here, the great sleep of forgetfulness saves people from disillusionment."

"But one can't go on like that indefinitely! There's no sense in it; one day is exactly like the other . . ."

"They don't know it. They live their one single day for ever. They are happy. Weren't you happy, too?"

"Yes . . . but, unfortunately, I remembered the day that went before!"

"You aren't yet accustomed to us. But you'll soon forget."

"God forbid!" I cried, "I can't do that, I don't want to!"

"In that case, you must leave this country."

"But Iza? What about her?"

"Iza will remain here. Do you want to see her old, grey, disillusioned? No, my dear sir, if you love her you'll have to stay here and conform to our rules."

"But I don't want to celebrate her name-day every day of my life and go on speaking about our engagement for ever!"

"All right. Choose a different day! It would rather complicate matters for me, though," and he pointed to the diagrams on the walls and to those strange instruments. "I have to coordinate the various wishes of our inhabitants in such a way that they are all of them happy, without being so at anyone else's expense. That is a difficult task, and it is impossible to arrange things satisfactorily for longer than one single day. There are wishes whose fulfillment would affect other people adversely; such wishes we can deal with only in the form of hopes. I might manage to arrange a different day for you — the one you regard as the happiest day in all your life."

"And that day would go on forever?"

"Yes."

"Good Lord! That would be the greatest misery!"

The old man laughed. "No, no, you would always experience it afresh as though it were the first time. Nobody here remembers the previous day, just as you don't remember where you were before your birth. Suddenly you find yourself here — and that is all. You'll know neither grief nor sorrow. You will have nothing but happiness

114

and hopes. You love Iza, don't you? Well, then, make up your mind! You can choose whatever day you wish: the day of your wedding, of some feast or revelry . . ."

"But what about work? I want to work, to get on in the world!"

The old man looked at me closely. "I have the impression that you're not particularly keen on working. But perhaps I might manage to provide you with some work on that day of yours. You will graduate from the university, enjoy your wedding feast, and hope that on the following day you'll achieve whatever else there is to be achieved by you. How about the wine? Wouldn't you like to drink it now?"

"No!" I shouted. "Is there no other way?"

"None."

"In that case, I don't want to!"

"You must leave, then."

"And what will happen to Iza?"

With an air of indifference, the old man shrugged his shoulders. "She'll go on waiting. Every day she will adorn herself with flowers, firmly convinced that you'll call on her the next day. And that will be her happiest day — her happiness will be in waiting."

"And I shall never come to see her?"

"Never."

"Never, never?" Despair clutched at my throat. My heart was torn by conflicting emotions, by longing and love, and by hatred for this old man. I thought of strangling him: perhaps it would break the spell which bound this town . . . I was just about to jump to my feet —

But at that moment he dexterously tapped my forehead with something that looked like a three-pronged golden fork. I fell and fell. . . and the old man burst into peals of feeble laughter.

And then I found myself standing outside the bungalow, gazing into the stars which shone with the light of eternity . . .

+ + +

"Well, that really was a crazy dream!" I remarked after an interval of silence.

"I've already told you that it wasn't a dream," Valdis said slowly.

"What was it, then?"

"Imagination, pure fantasy! Why should that disappoint you? Whether I dreamt it or actually experienced it — what difference would it make to the whole thing? How could the outcome possibly have been otherwise? Besides, I actually did experience it. Our thoughts are the only reality in this world where everything continuously shifts and changes. I was in One-Day Land, I was in despair — and I decided to escape. But I could not escape completely. . . . My worst days have remained with me, as a punishment."

"Why is that so?"

"Do you imagine that things don't repeat themselves? They do, only on a much wider scale. How are you going to prove to me that at some point, an eternity ago, we haven't already sat opposite each other as we do now — and that I didn't tell you exactly the same story? Or how can you prove that this very same situation won't be repeated after a few millions of years? Yes, true enough, our day lasts a bit longer. We experience both the fulfillment and the failure of our hopes. Sometimes it falls to my lot, sometimes to yours, some people experience everything, others must be content with less. And then we die and . . . forget. And everything begins all over again . . ."

"You've got an infernal way of reasoning," I remarked and quickly resorted to my glass of beer to convince myself that I was not dreaming some beastly dream.

"Perhaps I have. When I turned all those things over in my mind while looking at Iza's portrait on that autumn night, I felt that I had to leave the cottage at once. But I knew that some secret power would always draw me back again. Therefore I burned the print, averting my eyes. . . . Incidentally, that was also the end of my studies."

116

THE DOVE

IT WAS a clear, chilly morning in August 1944, steeped in the calm radiance peculiar to days that turn towards autumn.

Supervised by Germans of the Todt Organization, the group of men in the wood had begun to fell trees along the wide gravel road to obstruct the passage of tanks. Suddenly the rumbling of caterpillar tracks could be heard, and several men nearest the road raised their heads and listened.

"Tanks," one of them said.

A pale man with a bandaged foot smiled as he sat down under an alder bush. "Retreat! How will they advance again if we set up such grand obstacles all over the place?"

"Oh well, what does advance or retreat mean these days, anyway? You can only tell by your trousers what's front or back," another man retorted.

Grey shapes could now be seen through the gaps between the trees; they loomed up where the road climbed a hillock, and rapidly bore down upon the wood. The rumbling of their tracks grew louder.

A man dashed excitedly across the road, shouted something, and ran into the wood. He had flung his coat over his shoulder, and his knapsack, dangling from his hand, knocked against his legs and

117

hampered his progress. "Tanks, tanks!" he screamed as he ran past the foremost group of men.

"All right — tanks! So what?" one of them remarked peacefully.

"Russian tanks, with a star!" shouted the man. He stopped, as though the men's presence made this part of the wood safer than any other, and put on his coat and re-arranged his knapsack. At that moment the boom of two explosions reverberated above the wood, and there was a quick rattle of machine-gun fire. A small German defense post had been set up in the gravel pit by the little bridge; they were equipped with anti-tank rockets and had evidently tried to carry out their duties. Several men came running from that direction. Abandoning their saws, axes, and spades the working party — including the German supervisors — picked up their coats and knapsacks and took to their heels.

"*Die Organisation Todt ist doch tot,*" remarked the man with the bandaged foot, but there was no one left to hear him.

Applying the same tactics the Germans had used at the beginning of the war, the Russians now sent tanks forward wherever they sensed a weak spot in the crumbling body of the front line, not bothering about their rear and putting their new slogan into practice: "The Germans taught us to fight, but we'll give them a refresher course."

Daugavpils had fallen. Demoralized detachments of the German army dragged themselves along various roads towards Riga, their fighting capacity weakened by contingents of the older generation of reservists who were already doubtful about the outcome of the war. Civilians were rounded up, formed into working parties and set to work on entrenchments of which nobody knew for whom, or exactly at what place, they were required. Lines of newly dug trenches often fell undefended into the enemy's hands. But bridges were blown up, crops and houses were burned to the ground, and the roads were crowded with bewildered civilians in full flight.

Paying no attention to the men who had been erecting obstacles, the Russian tanks passed them by and continued on their way, and it was only then that panic broke out in earnest, aroused by the sudden shock and the din of the firing. The wood filled with fugitives, each concerned about his own safety, looking for shelter and hoping to make his way to Riga later on to rejoin his relatives. This working party consisted entirely of citizens of Riga; there were a few manual laborers among them, but mostly they were civil servants and employees of various firms.

Very soon the wood became empty along the road. The only person still remaining was the man with the bandaged foot. The unaccustomed jackboots had bruised his feet, the little toe on the left had begun to fester, and he could not get his foot back into the boot. This alone was sufficient reason for not keeping up with the others, but he did not even try to. He lay down on his stomach behind an alder bush and scanned the countryside around him. He saw several German soldiers from the gravel pit bolting for shelter into an unmown field of rye, and then everything was as quiet and empty as if nothing had happened. The tanks were not interested in individual people, he reasoned; in any case, they had gone, and probably there were no others to follow. "Never go where others go," he repeated to himself; it was a maxim life had taught him, though he could not remember where or when. He was not afraid, and he felt safest when he was alone. The presence of others only depressed him and deprived him of his independence. "Keep away from crowds, something always goes wrong there," he said to himself and calmly stepped out into the road which was gutted by the tanks; he eyed the sun, his knapsack slung over his back, a jackboot in his hand.

His thin, ash-blond hair was tousled; he had calm, regular features, except for his slightly wide mouth which habitually wore a faint smile and gave him a rather boyish look. On closer scrutiny, though, his face revealed a network of fine lines wrought by some secret suffering; he was not young any more. "What can happen to

119

me? Bah! Forward, always forward—that's the safest method of running away," he said to himself; he pushed the jackboot behind the straps of his knapsack and struggled across the ditch.

Limping a little, he made his way southward along its soft, grassy verge, but his apparently carefree air concealed a good deal of defiant despair. Walking in the sun, he soon felt hot, his foot hurt him, and he realized that he would not get very far. After this breakthrough of the tanks there was no chance of meeting anyone on the road who might give him a lift, no matter in which direction; but he was drawn on by the feeling that there was a farmstead somewhere close at hand. After a while he lay down in the shade to rest. Everything around was silent, warm, and peaceful. Above his head, a sunbeam penetrated through the branches of a pine tree, alighting on its needles with the sharp brilliance of a diamond and breaking up into many little rainbows. He suddenly felt faint with the beauty of this tranquil scene and with some inner yearning which overcame him whenever he was alone and let his mind wander.

"I'll go on my way and pass this branch, and perhaps I'll never see it again," he mused. "I may see other branches, but this particular one—no, never, never again." The thought gave him pain though it was not new to him; it had often crossed his mind when he found himself in places he had not seen before. The same thought had struck him at the sight of a little railway station, or cattle by the roadside, or a girl's kerchief; and every time he had felt inextricably bound, with no power on earth to release him—as water cannot be released from the compulsion to flow downhill.

"Have I grown old?" he asked himself. "Why should this make me sad? No matter where one goes, there'll always be something one sees for the last time. What an unpleasant thought . . ."

In the past he had coveted everything he saw for the first time. And when he groped among his memories his mind lingered over things he had carelessly passed by. He was restless, with a roving mind, capricious and fickle, a man who chased after sunbeams but

120

whose hand remained empty. Somehow, the Goddess of Fortune had granted him too much or too little of her bounty. He had achieved nothing, gained nothing. Yet he had no regrets; rather, there was a certain impudence in his attitude toward things which others clung to and valued highly — they did not seem worth his while.

In the last few years he had seen perish everything that people had attached themselves to. Apparently he had been right all along. But somehow there was a great deal of bitterness in having been so right, and it recoiled upon himself. He had nothing to lose in this thing called war — this whirlpool of feelings, earthly possessions, life, death — as a leaf driven by the wind has nothing to lose. He wanted least of all to stop anywhere, to get entangled with anything; he pursued something vague and intangible, something destined for him alone; but now he had begun to get attached to any trifle, even to the branch of a pine tree. The sunbeam had already moved on; the irritating pain in his foot brought him back to realities.

"Well, he argued, "millions of Chinese have had a hard life for thousands of years. Why be surprised if I don't get on too well either!"

Neither a believer nor an unbeliever, he was one of those who at times come to a sudden halt and wonder for an instant: Can this really be all that fate has in store for me? He had the impression that the whole world was holding its breath at this moment; close to death, everyone feels he is the one person on this earth who commands universal solicitude. But he was not prepared to die. His defiant mood returned, and he reviewed his position with all the stoicism he could muster. "There are sure to be farm buildings here. I'll walk in and wash my foot, and I'll drink milk and lie down to sleep, even if it has to be above the stables, and I'll be better off than all those cowards who scurried into the wood."

Limping, he continued on his way. He stopped by the edge of the wood and surveyed the sun-drenched countryside and the wrecked little bridge which seemed to have been the only victim in the short battle. He had not been mistaken: there was a farmstead; there even were two of them. The one on the hillock had been burned down, and smoke was still rising from its ruins, but the one in the valley had escaped destruction, probably because it was tucked away behind trees which screened it from the road. There were two faded, warped little wooden notice boards by the road leading to the farms, and he read: New Veveri — 0.5 km.; Old Veveri — 0.8 km. It was Old Veveri, then, to which the inscrutable course of this day's wanderings was to lead him. He increased his pace as though he were a guest expected at the farm.

It was a beautiful old farmstead; the yard lay in the shade of three lime trees, and there was an orchard lower down the slope. None of the buildings showed any signs of damage; they seemed to regard him with welcoming, kindly faces. There were marigolds, sweetpeas, and pansies blossoming in flowerbeds all along the front of the main building, and the pretty sand-strewn path was clean and newly raked. He stopped for a moment at the sight of this miracle, this complete unawareness of war or human anguish. The windows sparkled in the sun like pure silver, some hens strutted about in the yard, and a cat which had been sitting on the bench bristled up when it saw him and slid away round the corner of the house. But no dogs barked, and the doors of the cowshed, stable, and cart house stood ajar; he looked inside and saw that there were neither horses, cattle, nor carts; the only things left were old sledges and pieces of harness.

Without hope of finding anyone, he hammered with his fist on the closed kitchen door, but nobody answered. He rattled at the windows, but they gave him an empty stare. He thought for a moment, and then he carefully groped under the stones beneath the porch and — he was right — he found a key there, buried in the earth. Perhaps the owners of the farm had left it there out of long-established habit, or perhaps with the forlorn hope that they might come back again.

122

As though reluctant to give him access, the old door creaked in its hinges as it slowly opened and revealed a dark kitchen. There were bacon rinds in the frying pan on the hearth, and the remains of porridge in the saucepan. He walked through the rooms and found them in greater disorder than had appeared when he looked in through the windows. Chests of drawers, cupboards, and table drawers had been carelessly, hurriedly shut, but had not been completely emptied. In great haste, probably frightened by the fire on the neighboring farm, the people had obviously snatched up the most useful things — linen, clothes, food — and had taken as much as they could load onto a few carts. A clock was still calmly ticking on the parlor wall. There were crumpled sheets and pillows on the beds, but no blankets, and an old sheepskin coat hung in the corner by the wardrobe. In the larder he discovered half a loaf of bread, buttermilk, gooseberry jam, a little dish full of melted fat, a jar of pickled cucumbers, vinegar in a fluted bottle, and coarse grey salt on a saucer.

He walked through the rooms, ill at ease, feeling he ought to knock at each door before entering, though he knew it would serve no purpose since he was the only person here. Suddenly he began to enjoy being in sole possession. True, he was sorry for these people who had been forced to abandon in a few hours what had taken a lifetime to build up. Every trifling object left behind was part of a ruined life; it was sad to look at them. They reminded him of water plants cast out on the shore and withering into greyness, though a short time ago, in the depth of the lake, they had been of fantastic beauty, full of life and color.

But he did not wish for human company. He settled down comfortably in the kitchen and ate whatever came to hand, supplementing his meal with things out of his knapsack, and he grew calm and peaceful — though with that little touch of peevishness that comes to people who have dined well. Then he cleaned himself and bathed his foot; the sore was developing into an abscess, and he wrapped

123

a warm woolen cloth round his foot, closed the shutters of the back room, locked the door, and went to bed, covering himself with the old sheepskin coat. Smiling, he thought that this bed and coat very likely belonged to the master of the farm himself, and he fell asleep.

+ + +

He woke at the sound of distant firing, refreshed by sleep, alert, but slightly puzzled. His brain and his instinct of self-preservation sprang into action, sharp and quick. For a moment he sat on the edge of the bed, trying to grasp the situation and remember where he was. A series of vivid images flitted through his mind, showing him the progress of his wanderings that had ultimately led him right into the farmer's bed, and he sprang to his feet and pushed the window and the shutters wide open. The sky was clear, and the firing far off. The garden unfolded before him in the golden light of the afternoon: in the foreground, a tall tree with some rosy apples still on its topmost branches and, beyond the currant bushes, uniform rows of low trees with boughs drooping under the weight of large green and yellow apples.

"But where is the battle?" he asked himself. Had the front line moved on past the farm while he was asleep, and had it been consolidated? Tanks were usually followed by mechanized infantry units, and if that happened he would be in a tight spot. Suddenly he realized how easily he was moving about the room: his foot gave him no trouble at all. When he unwound the wrappings he saw that the abscess had burst. "Just at the right moment," he thought. "A bit of salve and some muslin, and I'll be able to march back." He needed warm water, but it was risky to light a fire: they might begin to shell the farmhouse. He tended the abscess as well as he could, praising himself for his foresight which had prompted him to put iodized salve and strips of muslin into his knapsack.

"There isn't really much difference between a man's body and his mind," he said to himself. "In fact, the mind is worse: some idea

124

takes root in you, and no amount of medicine can rid you of it."
With great difficulty he forced his neatly bandaged foot into the boot,
but it hurt when he tried to walk; he obviously would not be able
to march. "Nature, like fate, does everything at the right moment,"
he thought, and hunted up a pair of old wooden clogs in the kitchen,
slipped his feet comfortably into them and began to consider the
idea of marching in them.

"Principles are like wooden clogs," he remembered Bismarck's
saying, "useful when wading through mud, but no good if one has
to run." Well, he was not going to run; he would wait until the battle
was over and then try to slip away in the evening dusk. But the battle
had already ceased; there was no sound of firing when some air-
planes roared into view and disappeared again.

He spent some time going from window to window, expecting to
catch sight of the unknown victors and thinking it might be a bad
thing if he were found here on the farm. But the road and the sur-
rounding countryside remained quiet, and the orchard was suffused
with the tints of sunset. Waiting for darkness to fall, he packed his
knapsack and had a meal; finally he went out and stood on the
threshold. Pink clouds of dust suddenly rose from the road leading
up to the farm, and there was the rattle of cart wheels. What victors
were these who rode in carts? He stepped into the yard to have a
better look; recognizing German uniforms, he went back to the
house and stood in the door.

They were probably the office staff of some disorganized German
company of reservists. They drove into the yard in three carts, wag-
oners, rear-line men, with complete lack of military bearing, dusty,
tired, and altogether peaceable. He pushed his knapsack under the
bench and waited.

"Well, at last a human being," said the stout sergeant, extricating
himself from amid sacks and boxes of various sizes. "Anything to
eat?"

The man shrugged his shoulders. "I'm alone and ill."

"Never mind, we'll find something."

"You're welcome to it," he retorted and seated himself on the bench where the cat had been sitting when he entered the yard; like the cat, he bristled slightly, but he did not run away.

At first his presence seemed to embarrass the Germans, but gradually they became more free and easy: there was a thumping and clattering in the house, and from the hen coop came a swiftly stifled cackling.

A thin corporal came up to have a chat with him; it was obvious that he wanted to distract the attention of the master of the farm from what was going on inside the house. But the man on the bench was not talkative.

There was only one thing that interested him: "What has become of the Russian tanks?"

"Oh — smashed up, finished, our Rudel did for them!" They smoked the corporal's cigarettes. Yes, Rudel's dive bombers had destroyed the Russian tanks, as usual. The front was holding firm; it had been nothing to speak of, merely an unsuccessful breakthrough. And the corporal began to fidget, afraid that he had been talking too long: by not keeping an eye on his dispersed comrades he might have missed the chance of getting something good for himself.

The Germans, it seemed, were doing well for themselves. They discussed whether they should spend the night on the farm, but the sergeant said sharply No; and they all dispersed once more. At the backs of the carts they found room for a few hens with scraggy necks, and then they went off to look for something else, striding through the farm buildings and the yard with the curiosity and animation characteristic of people unrestrained by respect for another's property. They dragged out a few armfuls of towels and strips of carpet. The carts grew fuller. They were loaded with all sorts of trash: boxes, saucepans, chairs. But the latter were old and broken, and a soldier carried two new wicker chairs from the parlor into

126

the yard; when he noticed the man on the bench watching him he nodded understandingly and took the battered chairs from the cart: "Here's something to replace the others; they aren't really bad at all, but you must understand — war — we've no time to repair them," and he carried them back into the house. Thus they strode about, backwards and forwards, and at times it seemed as though they carried more into the house than out of it. They were newcomers to the front and had only just begun to taste the sweetness of looting; they were not experienced enough to distinguish between the useful and the useless.

At last silence descended on the farm buildings. All activity was transferred to the orchard, trees were being shaken, and then there was the sound of breaking branches. The loads on the carts grew bigger. The last rays of the sun streaked the sky with a calm, clear yellow. Loud voices and laughter rang out behind the apple trees in the garden, and the noise continued for some time. Several bees flew confusedly about the yard. The man on the bench raised his head and gazed thoughtfully in the direction of the garden; then he hid his knapsack among the firewood in the kitchen and went to see what was going on. The soldiers had discovered half a dozen beehives. Two men had put on gas masks and, their hands protected by leather gloves, busied themselves about the hives with knives and plates while the others stood laughing at a safe distance. It had long become clear to these soldiers that gas, regarded as the most dangerous weapon in the previous war, would not be a decisive factor this time; part of the army had been issued gas masks, but they signified just as little as the words *Gott mit uns* on the German soldiers' belts, also dating back to the previous war.

The man stopped about ten paces from the soldiers; a bitter taste rose to his mouth as he said: "At last you need gas masks."

"Perhaps you need one, too," one of the bystanders called out, throwing him a gas mask. He trod on it contemptuously and went straight towards the bee hives. The soldiers collected the honey-

127

combs they had taken from the hives, and stepped back. They were only rear-line men. "What a hellish day," the man thought, "what do I care about this farm and these hives."

But an inner voice said: There comes a time when you must go. And he went. He felt three, four stings on his neck and cheeks, but he went. He put his head into the open hive; there was a dark, quiet throng of bees, and as he had no idea what to do he arranged the remaining honeycombs in equal distances from each other. The bees crawled over his hands, and he hurt none of them, and none stung him. Some kind of friendship had sprung up between him and the bees, and it was stronger than any he had ever felt before. He replaced the roof on the first hive and then busied himself about the second one in the same manner, fully aware that this was not a bee-keeper's way of doing things but an action absolutely essential to himself. The soldiers stood about in silence, and then they began to drift back to the yard.

"Yes, yes," the corporal said, "bees know their master," and he slapped the man on the shoulder. "But it's war now, and who can tell when I'll get home again!" They all assembled in the yard, and the sergeant, climbing into one of the carts, pressed five Reichs-marks into the man's hand and said "Goodnight." Then the soldiers made ready to leave, convinced that Europe had never seen an army as honest as theirs.

"Perhaps you'd like to come with us?" suggested the thin cor-poral, but he stopped short when he saw the sergeant's forbidding look. For the sergeant had a secret that was not to be divulged to anyone: the German army was in retreat. This was obvious to everybody, but no one was allowed to mention it. Even in retreat this army was marching forward.

The man tersely said: "No!" And while he said it he felt that he was doing violence to his own good sense, that he ought to leave with the soldiers, that he would not get anywhere by himself with his sore foot, that he ought to scramble out of the invisible stream

128

which was sweeping him along. But the bee stings hurt him, and he felt as though he had received a slap in the face — aimed at himself and, through him, at the farmer with whose fur coat he had covered himself in the night.

He sat down on the bench and said to himself: "There are countries whose people could live happily if it weren't for droughts or floods, earthquakes, locusts, snakes, and crocodiles, oil or gold; but we have none of these, we only have the sunset and the sunrise and the fruits of our labor; this land of ours is so bright and clean that nothing impure wells up from it, only the sap of the birch trees in the spring, and it intoxicates none but those who have gazed deeply into the sun. . . . But all this is outweighed by the fact that we are situated between two gigantic nations who always imagine they are too small to be happy; and this is worse than droughts and floods, earthquakes, snakes, crocodiles, mosquitoes, and all the rest of it. It is so much worse that even I, who have never troubled myself about doing anything particular for this country, have to take to the road tonight."

But everything is equally safe and equally endangered in this world where, who knows for what reason, the swallow under the eaves and the ant on the path feel safer than the best-equipped soldier; where at times everything is decided by the momentary conjunction of a few events — a conjunction which seems accidental but flows from a will that is free precisely because it cannot foresee the consequences of the actions it has engendered.

The man with the knapsack could have slammed the door and walked away toward the north; but instead he invented reasons for staying yet a while. He closed the shutters, lit the oil lamp in the farmer's room, rummaged about until he found a dusty mirror, and extracted the bees' stings from his face. It had begun to swell, and for an instant his jocular mood returned. "A few more stings," he thought, "and this mirror would be too small to reflect my face." Well, never mind, at least he had saved the rest of the beehives.

129

Yet, hadn't he, too, come to this farm like a thief, to warm himself by the cold embers? And then something inexplicable had turned him into its protector.

Once more he walked through all the rooms and, compelled by a suddenly awakened love, began to put them in order. He carefully arranged the chairs in the corners, closed the drawers, picked up some books that had tumbled from the shelf and put them back in their places in a neat row; indeed, he was overcome by such an urge for tidiness that he went to look for a broom and swept the floors, which had been dirtied by the soldiers' boots. Now and then he glanced at the framed photographs on the walls: bearded men, women in blouses buttoned up to the throat and with hair swept upwards and tightly curled, a young girl in her long white confirmation dress, a hymnbook in her hands. Yet her eyes were full of the usual alluring promise of bliss — virtuous and wedded — and he gazed at her with pleasure. "Look," he thought, "these people have lived, and they still live, and I never knew of their existence, but now I am thinking of them!" He felt they were watching him at his work.

He went out again, stood on the threshold, and smoked and watched the darkness thicken. "Shall I go or shall I stay?" he wondered. There was coolness and peace in the dark shadows, but also some secret terror, mysterious like life or death. In his heart the vagabond struggled with the fugitive who had warmed himself under a stranger's roof and did not want to leave a shelter he had sought so long. He had attached importance to so many things in the course of his life but, after all, nothing had really been important. He had cast aside the women who loved him; they had either been too good to him or had wished him to be different from what he was, and he never wanted to stop anywhere, to make the least sacrifice. The others, the women for whose sake he had thought he might alter his ways, had not loved him. Or perhaps he was wrong, perhaps he could not think clearly, his face was so sore and swollen with the bee stings. . . .

130

He had always craved something unusual. But there was nothing unusual here: a forsaken farmstead, the same as a hundred others these days, and a fugitive who happened to have walked in. It was only in his mind that the unusual existed.

"I've never had a farm," he meditated, "and I'll never have one either — except tonight. I have entered perfectly free, and I shall leave perfectly free; but for one more night I'll cover myself with the farmer's fur coat. I am the protector of this farm, and to the best of my abilities I am its master. Only this one night! Then I'll go away, and I'll never again get entangled with anything; I'll care for nothing, and nothing will make me stop and linger — neither the branch of a pine tree nor other people's misfortunes. . . .

Perhaps, if I had known nothing but this farm and this girl in her confirmation dress, I might always have been as calm and peaceful as I am today. I might just as well have given up my life to her as to my doubts and my restlessness, my unsatisfied ambitions; my life would have completed the same circle, and at least I'd know why I am here at this place to which I have now come with no volition on my part. As things are, it seems as though this farm were the purpose of my existence."

Perhaps he was one of the last to feel that thoughts had no boundaries and that God had not yet chained Himself to two alternatives. He covered himself with the farmer's old fur coat, thinking that all things preserve the best that has been granted them: the fur coat — warmth, the human being — sleep.

+ + +

They came at daybreak, a patrol of five men, half-frozen, their uniforms saturated with dew; they must have been lying for an hour or so in the bushes, watching the farmhouse before venturing to enter it.

When the knock came on the shutters the man woke with a start and knew at once what it meant. The knock was like the sound of a bell he had been expecting all his life. Why had he closed the shutters? It had been childish — stupid to do so! He had wanted to sit in this house for a while by the light of the lamp. If the shutters had been left open they would never have thought of knocking.

No, that wouldn't have been much use either. He ought to have slept somewhere above the cowshed. But who could tell whether that would have made any difference. He ought to have left the farm yesterday. Why had he not gone? Because he had nowhere in the world to go.

For a moment he was overcome by the purely animal fear of the hunted man, and he even thought of fleeing. But his panic subsided; he passed his hand over his face, collected his thoughts, threw his coat over his shoulders, and went to open the door — slowly, deliberately, trying to regain his self-control.

The eyes of five men and the barrels of two automatics turned sharply upon him, and a voice shouted: "Hands up!" He did not raise his hands; he had never done so in all his life; the command insulted him. But the Russians were not so rigidly formalistic as the Germans. After one of them had hurriedly gone through the man's pockets and found nothing there, the command lost its force. They forgot having given it.

"You — the farmer?" one of them asked, but before the man had time to reply another soldier exclaimed: "Look, he's a proper fatface!" His face was so swollen with the bee stings that it had become perfectly round.

Two men went off to search the rest of the house while the other three remained with him in the farmer's room. "Have you seen any Germans?" asked the lieutenant.

"Yes, I have."

"Many?"

"Six."

"What's become of them?"

"They left yesterday."

132

"Where did they go?"

"They followed the road."

He had left his watch lying on the table, and now he saw it disappear into a man's pocket while he was being interrogated.

They searched the place; questioned him, taking him with them wherever they went; climbed to the attics, the lofts above the stable, and the cowshed. They had been brought up to trust nobody.

"Where are the others? Why didn't you run away?"

"That's none of your business," he retorted.

The Russian raised his head: "Listen, you — kulak! You've stayed behind in order to spy, haven't you?"

But at that moment they had reached the granary, and it attracted their attention because the door was locked.

"Why is it locked? Where's the key?" they asked.

"I don't know, I haven't got it."

"Of course you know! Get it at once!"

He realized that the moment had come to end this play acting, to tell them that he was not the owner of this farm but only a man who had been set to work digging entrenchments, that he had got here by chance, that he was sick and had been stung by bees; but his mouth stayed obstinately shut.

One of the men put his ear to the door of the granary and smiled cunningly.

"Where's the mistress of the farm?" he asked.

"She's not here."

"She's hidden herself, hasn't she?" With a crafty grin he hammered on the door.

"Open up!" the lieutenant called out.

"Listen, there's someone in there!" The soldier took hold of the man's collar and pulled his head down to the keyhole.

He was puzzled: there were strange sounds behind the door — a kind of rustling, a tripping about — and he could not make out what they meant. But it was clear that there was someone in the granary.

133

Was somebody really hiding there? One of the household, or perhaps a fugitive? That was a bad thing to do, just as stupid as his not leaving the farm.

"I don't hear anything," he said.

"So that's it, eh? You don't hear anything? Perhaps you'll hear better now!" The pistol butt struck his temple, lightly, it seemed, just a little knock, but he found himself sitting on the grass which seemed strangely green — never in his life had he seen such brilliantly green grass. He was violently sick; he saw them break the door in, and saw a blue pigeon suddenly fly out of the granary.

"Oh, the devils," said one of the soldiers, and he gave the man on the grass a look in which there was almost a hint of compassion. But that was exactly what the man did not need.

He raised his head and smiled. The five men understood nothing.

A pigeon, an ordinary pigeon, had found its way into the granary; perhaps it had entered by the hatch on the roof and scrambled through a gap between the planks of the ceiling, and then it had come upon some scattered grains of corn. This man was an eccentric who staked his life against the pigeon's.

He was happy; this moment set the crown on his useless existence. Holding his head high, he said: "What did you come here for, you scum? To capture doves?" The defiance of a race that had been beaten, humiliated, flogged, rose in him; it had furnished the vagabond with a sound contempt for his enemies. Contempt is harder to bear than hatred; at once the pistol was pointed at him, but at the same moment the lieutenant shouted, "Don't shoot!" He interfered not out of mercy but because they were reconnaissance men, ordered not to give themselves away unnecessarily.

The pistol was turned round, and the butt struck the man another blow, heavier than the first. "Even while we die we are happier than you are while you live," he sighed and surrendered to the dark stream that washed away his consciousness.

The sun rose slowly above the wood.

134

A LOVER'S LETTER

IT WAS already the third day of the third week of the third month that Vilnis had been in despair; he had not received any answer and did not know what to do. Perhaps this really was the kind of love that lasted six months, six years, sixty years? He had heard there was such a thing.

He was a trifle shallow, a trifle frivolous; this state of being in love affected him like some strange illness, and he tried to assure himself that it would pass and leave no aftereffects. He was in love, and yet he had kissed another girl, on purpose, so that his sweetheart should take notice of it. It had not been anything serious, merely an attempt to make her jealous and to prove his mettle: See what I can do if I feel like it!

Vilnis was in earnest as far as his girl was concerned, and she ought to have realized it. But she had apparently misunderstood him; everything had gone wrong. She had left for the country to stay with her parents, never answering his letters, and throwing his life into disagreeable confusion. In spite of his frivolity, Vilnis was a good judge of himself. "Perhaps she is right," he thought, "who can tell what is happening in my heart? Perhaps this is the kind of love that lasts six months."

Marksmen aim at a target with their more powerful eye and keep

135

the other shut. But with some men there is so little difference between the precision of the two that one eye is as good as the other. Vilnis always used both eyes when he admired the beauty of women; the idea of shutting one eye, and thus limiting his field of vision, would not have appealed to him at all. Yes, it was a nuisance: apparently one was required to concentrate on one particular girl and never look at any other. He was upset and unhappy — and this, strange to say, is a condition supposed to ensure a lover's ultimate happiness!

He sought solitude; he composed letters which remained unanswered. In the end it seemed to him that without an answer his life had no meaning.

How beautiful it would be if he could be lying in a coffin, his brow cold and white, and she, his great love, bitterly regretting not having answered his letters. The other girls he had kissed would also have to be there, of course. And each of them would place a bunch of flowers on his grave, in full view of her who had so grossly failed to understand him.

The only drawback was that he himself would not be able to see it. In time, he would be forgotten like all the rest in whose memory people erected monuments. If only one could sink into some semblance of death, which would make one more beloved, and then return to life, victorious!

Unfortunately, it is not given to mortals to cross this dividing line twice.

Vilnis felt very close to this dividing line as he lay on his couch on the afternoon of a bright August day; he had been dwelling on his misery, but finally he sat up, and wrote:

"In the park all the flowers are in bloom, even those whose names I neither know nor wish to know — for yours is the only name I can utter. If there is light about you, feel that it brings you my love. If a wind reaches you — just now it is gently ruffling my curtains — it is my love. If you are enveloped in darkness, remember: it is my love which languishes without light. And if there is neither light nor darkness about you, but only twilight — it is I! I am fully aware of the lack of truth in the life I have led hitherto, but truth is nothing compared to my prowess in telling lies, lies, and lies to win but one glance from your eyes. See how evil I am! But if you had the patience to read the meaning of my words correctly you would understand that this is a question of life or death."

When he had got thus far and re-read what he had written, Vilnis felt a certain satisfaction in having transferred part of his invisible burden onto the white sheet of paper. The effort had tired him, and he went out for a stroll in the park, thinking: "Is it really a question of death also?"

Some of his friends had noticed his melancholy and his desire for solitude; they happened to drive up that very moment, and they dragged him into their car. Among them was the girl he had kissed in order to spite his great love. She had no illusions about those kisses, but she was strong-willed and well able to make up her mind. Gradually, even without having seen Vilnis's despairing letter, she read the meaning of every word on his lips and in his heart — read it so correctly that Vilnis was amazed at his foolishness, which had made him reach for the moon and death while the sun itself was so close at hand. He was like soft clay waiting for the master's hand to mold him. Now he was molded by this girl's love, though it took her longer than it had taken the girl who never answered his letters.

In the meantime a mischievous gust of wind had carried off his letter and deposited it among the flowers in the park — whose names he did not know.

+   +   +

Emilia was out for a walk, giving her little boy an outing in his perambulator. Nothing unusual ever happened in her life. She picked up the letter the wind had blown into the park, and read it. Then she sat down on a bench, pushed the perambulator into the half-

137

shade so that the baby should be warm and yet protected from the sun's shining into his eyes, and she read the letter once more. With a little laugh, she looked about her: which of the people here could have lost such a letter? But the park was empty; most people were still at work. The odd mixture of poetry and nonsense in the letter rather moved her. She put it into her handbag, went home, and prepared her husband's dinner; she would show him the letter, and she even thought of the remark she was going to make: "Look, you've never written me a letter like that!"

But her husband was in a bad temper; one of the clerks at the bank had made a stupid mistake, and he felt personally responsible. He quickly swallowed his dinner, told her all about his vexations, and seated himself at the writing desk to compose a report for the bank manager from which it would clearly emerge that he himself was after all in no way to blame.

Emilia cleared the table and put the little boy to bed; then, in rather a bad temper herself, she sat down by the lamp opposite the writing desk and read the letter for the third time. She read it in such a way that her husband should notice she was perusing something interesting. But he merely turned an absent-minded eye on her, absorbed in the search for greater coherence in the sentence he was about to write, blind to her pretty dark-brown frock, her figure, her earrings, and blind to the fact that she was reading a letter.

Finally she grew bored with it all. With a brusque movement she switched off the lamp, hid the letter in the drawer of her dressing table, and went to bed.

After that evening, an invisible worm seemed to keep gnawing at the foundation of their family life.

Emilia's husband was a decent, sensible fellow who planted the customary kiss on his wife's cheek after breakfast and after dinner, and who regarded his family as such a stronghold of all the virtues that there was room neither for improvement nor glorification. He was an attentive husband; now and then he noticed that the heel of a shoe was going to pieces or that his wife was getting tired of a certain dress. "Buy yourself something," he said one time, producing a couple of banknotes. His wife brightened up and exclaimed: "Would you like me to buy a dress with a low neck and the new narrow waistline? What do you think? And my hair . . . would you like me to cut it a bit shorter? Even old women get themselves up like young girls these days."

"Well, well, what next!" her husband laughed. "Everything you wear is nice! So far, everything suits you . . ." And he left the house, thinking that nothing but a few minor touches of diplomacy stood between him and the post of assistant bank manager.

But the invisible worm did not stop gnawing. Emilia sometimes flared up about nothing at all, broke a plate or a coffee cup, bought herself crazy hats and thumped something on the piano that sounded like waltzes; in the middle of the day and sometimes in the evening, too, she went to cafés to meet former school friends, so she said, and her husband had to stay at home and mind the baby. The good-natured man put up with it for quite a while, pretending not to notice these changes. In the past it had never entered his mind to ask any questions, and he realized it would be humiliating to start asking now — and what, exactly, was he to ask her?

Finally, on one of his lonely evenings, he felt that things had gone too far; this gave him the necessary justification for doing a little research. First of all he looked through his wife's old album which contained photographs of her schoolmates; judging by their youthful portraits, they were a pack of fools. He thought of his own acquaintances, some of whom were interesting people; they seemed decent enough — but who could tell! Then he went through his wife's drawers and found all sorts of trinkets, ribbons and pins, advertisements cut out of newspapers and magazines, letters from women friends, carnival photographs in which he was greatly astonished to see himself with rather a leer on his face.

"This is the small, trifling world in which she lives!" he thought,

139

finding it distasteful to have to delve into it. But at the bank where he worked, too, surprising things sometimes came to light when the auditors came unannounced.

Under the little casket which contained her amber necklace was Vilnis's letter. At last!

He read it several times, and the post of assistant bank manager suddenly lost all importance. Still, in spite of the letter, his work was extremely important. Yes, he would show them that here was someone superior to that imbecile. One thing was certain: he would keep his son and bring him up himself. The divorce would be unpleasant, but he would endure it as he'd endure having a bucket of icy water emptied over him. How mistaken one could be about women! He tried to remember a few he had passed by. Maybe they were better?

He paced about the room, now and then stepping into the nursery, folding back the blanket and listening to the little boy's breathing. When his rage had burnt itself out he began to think of the situation as simply sad. He would be subtle, polite, and distant — not overbearing. That would be his approach.

He seated himself by the lamp, Vilnis's letter in his hands, and waited for his wife to return.

Emilia entered, threw down her gloves, removed her hat, and went into the nursery. She re-appeared, looked at herself in the mirror and finally noticed her husband. She had never seen him sitting so nonchalantly in the rocking chair, reading; obviously something must have happened to him.

"Have you been promoted?" she asked coldly.

"It depends how one looks at it," and he lowered Vilnis's letter to his knees so that she should see it.

Emilia was a little frightened. She had long been waiting for this moment, but now she found it far from pleasant.

"You read my letters?"

"You can always read mine; there's nothing in them that would interest you."

140

"Is this letter more interesting?"

"No, but who's written it to you? What elephantine brainlessness! Of course, without a heading, without a signature. Clever, eh? I'd just like to see his face!" and he rose to his feet.

"I found it in the park, I don't know who wrote it," Emilia confessed sooner than she had intended, seeing the dangerous look in her husband's face.

"In the park, indeed! The things that grow in parks nowadays! — Lies, lies, nothing but lies! And it's winter now, have you been in the park at all?"

"Such letters can be written also in winter," Emilia rejoined. "But it was in the summer when I found it; I wanted to show it to you the same evening, but you were worried about the junior clerk, you were writing, and you had no time to look at me. You could have found the letter any day; sometimes I put it under my handbag, but you never looked at it, you never noticed how old it is . . ."

"The letter?"

"No, the handbag," Emilia sobbed.

Her husband sighed and examined the handbag. "It looks all right to me, I've had my purse for five years already."

"But the money inside it changes; here nothing changes, nothing at all, only the morning and the evening . . ."

He gazed at her thoughtfully for a while, and almost laughed. "All right, we'll buy a new handbag and anything else you want."

"Oh, but I want nothing, nothing, nothing . . ."

"Why didn't you show me the letter later, the next day?"

"You never have time, and I have other things to think about."

"Well, then — have you tracked this lover down?"

"Tracked him down? What do you mean?"

"I mean, don't you know even now who has written the letter? All the flowers are in bloom . . . telling lies, lies, and lies to win but one glance from your eyes. Really, I've never read anything quite so stupid!"

141

"So you think I'm not worth it? Would you never tell lies for my sake?"

Her husband contemptuously flicked at the letter.

"This fool has turned the meaning of words upside down; of course there is truth in love!"

"And is there none in the letter? I want flowers, a new handbag, kind words — and lies, if kind words aren't forthcoming . . ."

He raised his wife's wet face from the cushion, wiped her tears, and murmured thoughtfully: "Yet, you loved him, didn't you?"

"Yes — only, he doesn't exist."

After this, her husband made it a rule to give Emilia flowers, to present her with a new handbag every year, and to talk pleasantly to her more often than he had done in the past. In the evenings he sometimes gazed thoughtfully at his wife — a charming, agreeable creature whose neckline, hemline, hair style, and earrings changed every year — and he quietly pondered the question: "Is she truthful, or does she tell me lies?"

The letter from Vilnis had been returned to its accustomed place under the casket with the amber necklace. The husband found it there and put a match to it, enjoying the spectacle of the letter slowly turning to ashes.

Emilia looked for it among her trinkets and said pleasantly: "My lover's letter seems to be missing. Have you done anything to it?"

"I don't know . . . no, I don't think so. Oh yes, I remember, I burned some old papers yesterday, perhaps, among them . . ."

"I know it by heart, though you're no good at telling lies!" she retorted, trying on a pair of new earrings by the mirror. "In the park all the flowers are in bloom, even those whose names I do not know — for yours is the only name I can utter. If there is light about you, feel that it brings you my love. If a wind . . ."

"Oh, stop, stop!" her husband interrupted her. "I also know it by heart! And if you want me to lie to you I might say that I hate you, but you know it's a lie!"

142

# A DELICATE MISSION

DAY followed day, smoothly and uneventfully, with nothing to distinguish one from another. Arnis Grants had some time in his life become disillusioned and had reached the conclusion that it is best not to interfere in other people's affairs — if one keeps to himself people leave him alone, particularly if one holds a position that does not arouse envy. He worked as a librarian; it was a quiet, peaceful occupation, not likely to be interrupted except perhaps by an outbreak of fire. But one morning his aunt paid him a surprise visit at the library.

"To what do I owe this honor?" Arnis asked sarcastically. "I haven't any books on dreams. They've all been taken out by our readers."

"There you go, always at your stupid jokes," his aunt retorted furiously.

"Have you any better ones, then?"

Arnis remembered only too well that his aunt owned a large house and a grocery store, and that she had always given him a slice of dry bread for breakfast when, as a schoolboy, he had lived with her. No doubt bread is very good for one's health — even if one has to eat it without butter.

"Arnis, you know that Ilmars has a high opinion of you. You have the cleverest brain in our family."

143

"Oh, is that so? Till this moment I always thought that it was you who had that distinction."

"Well, yes, but not in such matters as these. Ilmars hasn't got anywhere yet, he hasn't finished his studies, and now the unfortunate business with that lady . . ."

"What lady?"

"You're only trying to pretend that you don't know! It's the talk of half the town."

"My dear aunt, I belong to the other half."

"That's why I'm telling you all about it!" Her eyes flashed with anger. "Don't imagine I have any selfish motives. It's just that I can't see any happiness for Ilmars in it. I've already found out a few things about her: she is a janitor's daughter, a small-part actress, and was married to the prompter of the theater — he was a drunkard — they were divorced, the child died. Now she is a dressmaker, keeps a fashion salon, calls herself Lilita Alpha. What do you think of such an addition to the family? Ilmars often comes home drunk, and now he tells me he has proposed to this lady. Fine kind of lady, I must say! She pays actors' and painters' bills at taverns. With that type of woman, Ilmars will end up with no clothes to his back. He'll do nothing but go the round of the taverns with her and lie about in the gutters, drunk."

"Wait a moment," Arnis said slowly. "Since she is a dressmaker it isn't likely that Ilmars will walk about with no clothes on, you know. And she wouldn't pay these young fellows' bills if they weren't too poor to pay for themselves. It is a sad state of affairs from their point of view, but would we be willing to pay their bills, you and I?"

"Arnis! One doesn't associate with such people! Besides, she is several years older than Ilmars. He's fallen under her spell — that's what happens when young men meet women with loose morals. It will pass. Only it shouldn't be allowed to get out of hand; one ought to be firm with him. You know how it is when a boy grows up without a father. I am helpless, he won't listen to me. Couldn't you speak

144

to him, couldn't you ask him to consider very seriously what he is doing? He's still got his whole life before him." His aunt was in tears, and Arnis promised to do what he could.

Nevertheless, he doubted whether he was the right person to undertake such a delicate mission. A straight talk with Ilmars might undermine his own authority for good. The boy was ten years younger than himself and had on occasion given in to Arnis when he tore his notions to shreds with wittily sarcastic arguments or merciless contempt. But how was he to tackle the problem of love? He could not possibly stoop to collecting gossip about Lilita Alpha.

Arnis remembered that he had once met this dark-haired, dangerous-looking lady at a café in the company of Ilmars and some artists. He had sat at their table without speaking a word, and had soon taken his leave. When he went to the cloakroom to get his coat he had glanced back over his shoulder and had noticed that the smile was fading from her face. The look in her eyes had haunted him all the way home, and he had passed his hands over his face as though to brush something away, saying to himself: I'm too old for this sort of thing!

After this incident Ilmars had now and then put in a hurried appearance, urging him to call on Lilita Alpha. "Come with me, and you'll see what a wonderful woman she is! She understands everybody — artists, writers, everyone — oh, what a soul she has! I promised to bring you along; she has invited you!"

"Thank you. Another time, perhaps," Arnis had said. The youthful expressions "wonderful woman" and "soul" grated on his ear.

It suddenly struck him that he had forgotten to ask his aunt whether Ilmars's proposal of marriage had been accepted. In his opinion, it was not necessary to try to find out absolutely everything about a person. This would only complicate matters. It was sufficient to know something of a person's motives or intentions, which provide better insight into people's characters than all the gossip about their private lives.

145

From day to day, Arnis Grants postponed his investigation into Lilita Alpha's intentions. But finally, on a Saturday, he screwed up his courage and set out to call on her.

He had never liked the idea of calling on strangers and asking questions. The awkwardness of his mission made him quite timid. He rang, barely touching the button of the bell. Then he pulled himself together, rang again, louder than before, and waited. There was no movement behind the door; he rejoiced at the thought that the fateful meeting had to wait until some other time. Arnis was already on his way down the steps when the door opened behind him. Taken off guard, he had no time to adopt a suitable expression, and he realized that the face he presented to Lilita Alpha displayed an unprepossessing combination of emotions. She glanced at him quickly; for a moment she looked profoundly thoughtful and sad, and this made her uncommonly beautiful. It was the same transformation he had seen in her face when he left the café.

Then she smiled.

"Mr. Grants! What a surprise! Do come in. You must forgive me, I haven't had time to change into a dress. My ladies don't usually come for fittings at this time of day, and I've been trying to catch up with my work."

She pulled the collar of her long housecoat closer about her neck.

"No, no, it is up to me to apologize for this intrusion! I happened to be passing . . ."

Lilita Alpha hung up his coat and tossed his hat skillfully onto a hook.

"I did not know that you frequented this neighborhood,"she remarked as she led the way into the sittingroom, stopping for a moment by the hall mirror and brushing a speck of powder from her nose with her little finger. "Your cousin tells me that you live far away and are very busy."

"Ilmars? Does he come here often?"

"Yes. Hasn't he told you? Why did you never come with him?

146

Surely, it ought to be your business to know what company he keeps.'"

The irony in her voice was unmistakable, but Arnis Grants made no answer. He was reserving his strength for a more serious skirmish.

"Do sit down!" She motioned him to an easychair and curled up like a kitten in the chair opposite, carefully covering her ankles with the hem of her housecoat so that only the tips of her shoes and a little strip of white skin remained visible.

"And now tell me what is worrying you!"

"I haven't any worries of my own," Arnis tried to be jocular, "but I sometimes make a nuisance of myself to other people."

"When you first rang the bell you let go at once, but the second time you pressed the button a little longer. You've got something on your mind that is difficult to put into words. You tried out my doorbell, but you'd have been relieved not to find me at home. Am I right?"

"You seem to have plenty of experience with doorbells."

"Yes, up to a point. A tramp would first have given a loud ring and then a fainter one because hope fades quickly. But excuse me for a moment, I'll go and make some coffee. And surely you wouldn't refuse a few sandwiches? Also, I'd better change into a dress even though I opened the door to you in a housecoat."

Arnis examined the pictures on the walls. No doubt they had been painted by those penniless young artists whose bills at public houses were paid by this "lady," as his aunt had told him. Still, the pictures were good. He had a look at the photograph albums, and there, with lengthy dedications sprawling across the foot of their portraits, he discovered several of his acquaintances — violinists, cellists, actors. For some unknown reason these men and their conceit infuriated him. "Oh well, it's none of my business," he argued, calming down. "Everyone tries to look the man he wants to be. It's only natural."

Lilita returned, very elegant in a dark purple dress, and put a tray with a dozen tiny sandwiches on the glass-topped table. Arnis Grants

147

was not particularly hungry, but he secretly consulted his watch and found that it had taken her a bare twelve minutes to change into her dress, make coffee, and prepare the sandwiches. Being a bit of a cynic, he judged she had spent four minutes in the kitchen and eight minutes in front of her mirror. This quickness and efficiency pleased him; his heart warmed towards her.

He ate and drank, not forgetting to thank his hostess for the charming repast — delightful to both his eye and his palate — she had set before her unexpected visitor.

"I'm beginning to understand Ilmars," he said. "You bewitch a man in no time at all, and your spell works even when you aren't there in person. Yes, a day without you might easily appear dull and empty."

"Would you want me to be different — for Ilmars' sake?"

"No, no, that wasn't quite what I meant, Mrs. Alpha," Arnis stammered.

"My name is Abramsons," Lilita suddenly interrupted him. "I use Alpha for business purposes."

"Just as I thought — alpha, beta, gamma — Greek letters! Who gave you the idea?"

"Why should I go to other people for ideas? I simply began from the beginning when I started to lead an independent existence."

Arnis looked at her with heightened curiosity. She seemed a little agitated; her slender fingertips danced over the arm of her chair as though drumming some disconnected tune, and there was a slight frown on her brow.

He remembered the mission he had rashly undertaken on behalf of his aunt.

"May I ask how old you are?"

"Twenty-nine," she laughed. "But I fail to see the connection."

"Ilmars is twenty-five."

"Didn't I tell you that there's something worrying you? Would you like another cup of coffee?"

148

Arnis shook his head.

"Forget your worries and tell his mother that I have no intention of marrying her spoiled little darling. How old are you?"

"Thirty-five. But what has that got to do with it?"

"You ought to have acquired some wisdom — by now!"

Arnis Grants smiled and glanced at his watch, purposely misunderstanding her remark.

"Oh, I'm sorry! I wasn't hinting that it was time for you to go!"

Lilita Alpha-Abramsons threw a cushion on the floor and sat down at his feet, her arms about her knees, and she bestowed a look upon him that would have turned even the stump of an old pine tree into a sweetly melodious harp.

"Now you have cleared up everything as far as Ilmars is concerned. I think he ought to be told."

"How do you mean to set about it?"

"Well, we might leave the house together, you and I, and pin a note for Ilmars to the doorbell. He said he'd call tonight with some friends. I don't allow him to come by himself. It's different with you, of course — you are much more serious than Ilmars and, besides, I didn't expect you to come alone."

"That's a strange rule you've introduced! Why didn't you simply tell Ilmars not to call on you at all?"

"Try to guess why I didn't! But I might at least write him a note about tonight. Only, I honestly don't relish the idea of roaming about in the dark streets all alone just in order to make your mind easy about your cousin."

Arnis suggested that they might both go to a café.

He glanced over Lilita's shoulder as she wrote: "I am sorry, but it so happens that I won't be at home tonight."

"Perhaps you'd like to add some remarks of your own?"

"No," Arnis said, embarrassed, "it's all right as it stands!"

It was a warm evening, fragrant with the scents of spring. Young leaves were budding on the lime trees along the boulevards, and in

149

the park flanked by the university and the opera house there were exotic trees in full bloom. Each had a label with its Latin name affixed to it, but on this particular evening nothing was further from the librarian's mind than scanning labels or reading anything whatever.

He stood beside Lilita on one of the bridges across the canal; leaning over the parapet, they gazed at the moonlight on the slowly flowing waters and at the shadows cast by their heads until the two shadows merged into one.

They wandered from bridge to bridge and from bench to bench, kissing while the moon shone overhead and the distant cafés gradually went dark and closed for the night.

Toward morning they parted by Lilita's front door.

But in the meantime Arnis had actually become jealous of Ilmars and had tried to discover why his cousin should have been allowed to call on Lilita so often.

"I always hoped he would bring you along one day! He'd promised, but it never seemed convenient — you live so far away, and you are always so busy. And finally I hoped that his mother might ask you to speak to me."

"That was rather a complicated plan for a campaign!"

"Well, darling, aren't you rather a complicated sort of person?"

Arnis Grants walked home, dizzy with happiness and meditating on his maxim: one need not know everything about a person, it is sufficient to know something of his motives or intentions.

After a few days he wrote to his aunt.

"Dear Aunt, Ilmars has been saved. Nobody can save me. I am going to marry Lilita. The boy has perfect taste, but he is obviously too young. I hope he will get over it!"

150

CORDA

DOCTOR Varklajs always walked silently and carefully, in soft F major. But the asphalt pavement, leading from the gate of the front garden to my entrance door, echoed his footsteps: F, A, C, F, A, C . . . At my threshold he would sound an E flat and hesitate for a moment over an unresolved seventh chord, wipe his feet — it was the resolution — in D and a threefold repetition of B flat. He would then ring the doorbell in a piercing C sharp. I would open the door, we would greet each other — a modulation — and presently we would enter the austere key of B flat major.

With a view to amusing him, I would play the theme of his arrival and, after he was seated in an armchair, strike a full, rich B flat chord; but whenever he was in low spirits we would change over to D minor.

"Let's have some red wine, Rait," he would suggest. "You should drink red wine; it stimulates the circulation of the blood and will give you an appetite. I myself probably shouldn't drink it any longer, but what can I do if I like it?"

I poured him a glass of Burgundy warmed to body temperature, exactly as he liked to have it. He touched the glass the way he would feel a patient's pulse, inhaled the wine's fragrance, and said: "It's

151

just right when the glass is at body temperature and you don't feel it when you touch it. Let us drink!"

I followed his example, adding: "Burgundy stimulates my imagination and then makes me sleepy, or — if I drink some more — it makes me sad, but it doesn't at all affect what you call my appetite."

"You must walk in the park for at least an hour, preferably in the morning, looking at the beauty of the foliage and the sky, before you settle down at the piano for practice or composition."

"That's what I do, although afterwards I'm overcome with fatigue and thus lose a few hours. I can only compose in the evening; the morning looks too real."

"You are neurasthenic, with small reserves of energy. Haven't you got anything in the house to eat?" he asked after the third glass. "Bring me some brown bread and salt!"

I did as he asked. "I'm really very sorry, but I can't offer you any butter. In accordance with your advice I have a cellar full of Burgundy, but I forgot all about food. Besides, I never cook anything. But you can have brown bread and salt."

"That goes very well with wine," he said appreciatively. "Indeed — wine, bread, and salt are the symbols of human existence, culture, and simplicity."

He fell silent for a moment, looking through the window into the gathering twilight.

"And now you are probably considering the most delicate manner in which to tell me that you think I'm looking overwrought?" I broke the silence.

"I have told you so after each of your concert tours, because you are living in a sort of fever which might impair your artistic faculties — something neither of us would particularly like. Do you still see her?"

"You mean Corda? Thanks for inquiring . . . I see her whenever I least think of her — when, following your advice, I have been out walking in the park and come back and sit down at the piano. I

152

cannot evoke her deliberately. But she will appear suddenly — almost as suddenly as Miss Gita, whom you send for a walk in the park at the time when I'm supposed to be there," I laughed.

Doctor Varklajs took a sip from his glass. "Rait, you are very much mistaken when you think that we are plotting against you. Gita loves you. I simply told her the time when you are out in the park. Do you dislike her?"

"I wouldn't say that. Her profile looks splendid against the background of the pond when she is feeding the swans. It might even gratify you to know that I have kissed her."

"I never dared hope for that much; you are progressing toward a new symphony."

"I am afraid not . . . I don't like human flesh. She has a beautiful, delicate skin, but I hate hers as much as I do my own. I don't like my body; it very often disgusts me — in fact, everything connected with it does, for that matter!"

"It is because you are living alone in a world of your own. The body, the qualities of which are common to us all, reminds you of the outer world which you hate, for some reason or other."

"My dear doctor," I said, "music knew the wonderful laws of counterpoint and harmony when medicine was still subsisting on magic words and herb infusions."

"But, incidentally," I went on, "the world is hateful. Usually all disasters and misfortunes are blamed on mad or drunk people though none of these is able to invent anything so wretched as human existence for the wretchedness of which the responsibility rests with the sensible, the ambitious, the covetous, and the devout . . .

"I know, you come to see me in order to observe an interesting case. As a physician, you are interested in finding out how the body works when you cut it open; but have you ever reflected on what happens to the mind when you put it to sleep — possibly never to wake up again? Sometimes I feel an unreasonable fury when I see your inquisitive face. Essentially, your interest in me is equally un-

153

reasonable; once you are dead you will no longer be a physician but merely the corpse of an honored physician. Everything we long for is outside of what we are. Love, ideas, everything that governs our pleasure or displeasure is somewhere else — not in this room. The melancholy D minor triad which I am now striking on the piano resembles you with drooping arms: D is the left one, A the right one, and in the center is F — your head. Now I fill your glass with wine, you drink of it: I've added a sharp to F, your head, and it is now a triad in D major. Your mind is growing more optimistic, possibly to the point of your wanting to sing. Do, by all means! I'm going to accompany you."

"Thanks, my hour for singing has not struck yet." The doctor quickly crossed his legs, and continued: "Rait, you are unfair to me. I'm fond of you and your music, despite my being a physician. You hate the body, that's why it is covered with clothes. But we have no other means of communicating with each other; I simply could not come and see you if I had no body. Or do you think I could turn up in a different way — as Corda does?"

"Why not? In a way you are present even when your body is resting on your bed; I'm thinking of you, although you're trying to forget your patients.

"When I was still in the orphanage, I used to wake up in the morning twilight and see a severe-looking grey man standing at my bedside. He would stand between my bed and the boy's next to me, looking out through the window where just at that moment the rosy morning was emerging from the greyness outside."

The doctor put both his feet on the floor, resolving the second: F-G turned into E-G. He had become interested. "I hope you're not going to deceive me," he said, "and tell me something out of a bad story, such as children should not be allowed to read."

"Oh no, I was eight years old. I had only read travel stories and a fairy tale about how a stupid ram, by running down a hill, killed the clever wolf. Such things do not happen; they only show what

154

great care our educational institutions take to conceal the truth as long as possible . . .

"The grey man was the size of a real man; as a matter of fact, he was the founder of the orphanage, at whose portrait we looked every day, during mealtimes, in the large hall."

"It sounds plausible," the doctor remarked.

"It is interesting that from the portrait he had developed into a full-size human being. My first reaction was fright. I half closed my eyes, but very soon, out of sheer curiosity, I opened them again. He was still standing there. Then I shut my eyes for quite a long time; when I opened them again he was no longer there. The sun had risen, and it cast a wide strip of light on the floor between the beds."

"Did you tell anybody about this apparition?"

"No, I was not scared; the apparition did not do me any harm. And, as you know, children will not disclose their most intimate experiences. Afterwards, I was ill for quite a long time. I had a high fever which at times subsided only to return and seize me again when everybody thought I was better. I don't remember our doctor's being able to diagnose this disease. Occasionally, I would see wonderful sights: fields and meadows, hills and castles, toward which I advanced, gliding up invisible stairs, but then everything would vanish . . . The most unpleasant and ever-recurring sensation was that of my having huge bulky hands in which something always seemed to be forming and swelling, without, however, my feeling what it really was."

"You didn't tell anybody about this either?"

"Certainly not. Telling would have served no purpose; medicine was not yet sufficiently advanced at that time. Nor is it now, for that matter. Our existence is like a thousand-footed and thousand-scaled reptile. A scale will die — and the senses cease to function. This scale is buried to the accompaniment of hymn-singing and talk of eternity. But at times, because of a strange freak of nature or sheer neglect, it will happen that a ligament is not completely severed. If

155

we remember yesterday, why might we not sense tomorrow and distant events, distant thoughts? Every single thing in the universe is in contact with another, only we lack the faculty for sensing this. Perhaps that is just as well; otherwise we might be worse off than we are now. Anyhow, the world no longer seems so grand as it did when we were still children. It looks rather pitiful; there are only transient raptures or, rather, strange poignancies to which we cling . . ."

"Have you any other recollections of childhood? Of your infancy?" the doctor asked.

"The earliest is of a sort of light. It must have been a house on fire, a conflagration such as I have subsequently often seen, stopping whenever I passed the place of disaster."

"How strange . . ." the doctor murmured. "Have you got some more Burgundy?"

"As much as you like, I'll go and fetch some from the cellar right away."

When I returned, the doctor was trying to strike a chord in D minor on the piano — varying it with one in D major — possibly musing on where the clue to the wonderful difference of harmony, caused by changing from a white key to a black key, might lie hidden.

He turned abruptly from the keyboard, looking at me, and sat down again in his armchair.

"Thinking about your childhood, Rait, and the apparition you have seen, I remember the Latvian popular tales about ghosts. In these, it often happens that someone falls ill after seeing a spook, while actually the seeing of apparitions is the result of illness."

"You are quite right, doctor! And hasn't humanity been ailing for centuries already? One might even say since the day of creation. Perhaps you are one of the ghosts created by the imagination of mankind?"

The doctor smiled. "Ghosts don't drink Burgundy! But tell me something about Corda."

156

"Well, after returning from a concert tour, I felt quite exhausted, yet I couldn't sleep. I sat down at the piano and, quite leisurely, began to strike a single key — A — in varying degrees of loudness. There are some compositions of Chopin's, you know, which begin on one note, as if reflecting on what could be developed out of it. That note is like a mysterious bell, preceding the rise of the curtain and the subsequent appearance and flutter of the spirits of sound let loose. . . . I was thinking: How could one single sound cause such a strange thing as people coming together to listen to a concert, whispering together, applauding, and parting, as if something had happened in their lives, while nothing had really happened at all? Only time had passed by. Worried by these reflections, I had half closed my eyes without, however, falling asleep; when I opened them again I saw her appear — as a light, as the features of some immaterial face for the sake of which you would be ready to give yourself wholly and entirely. As I looked at her more intently, she vanished. I had before me a sheet of a composition bearing the annotation *una corda* which, as you know, means that you have to apply the soft pedal which causes the padded hammer to touch only one of the three strings tuned to the same pitch, thus softening the sound; that's why I named her Corda."

"Did you have any premonition that the apparition might materialize as — or rather personify — a female being?"

"I haven't thought about that, but if you ask me I admit it might be a woman."

The doctor gave a laugh. "It is your art and your erotic dreams that condense into this apparition. But, surely, Corda doesn't exist?"

"Why do you take that for granted? Are you sure that you yourself are actually here, and that your soul is not drying in hell to serve as a handkerchief for the Devil?"

I refilled the doctor's glass.

"An Oedipus complex . . ." he muttered.

"I don't remember my mother . . ."

157

"That's exactly why this longing is haunting you."

"Language is apt to debase things. If I had told you that Corda was not a woman, and that she showed signs of a beard, you would say that I have probably been concentrating too much on paintings of Christ and the Apostles by the old masters, and that the erotic element in me is sublimated into the religious. Is God in the church when it is empty? We do not know. When we gather together we try to shape our God out of the feeling, big or small as it may be, which each of us takes along with him on a Sunday. You may give things their names, but that does not mean that they become simpler for that. You haven't got a complex of your own; you just represent the complex of health and simplicity, don't you?"

"My dear Rait, you are unfair again. God has in like manner conceived both you and me. But you are trying, as it were, to reach for too high a shelf which neither of us can take down or lift up. But there's a smell of smoke in the room, haven't you noticed?"

"No, I haven't — it's only an emanation from your vague words. Sometimes I can't find sleep at night; I shut my eyes, and a bright spot flares up in front of me. It'll veer, dissolve, and, finally, turn into contorted, hideous human faces. Perhaps they are the faces of some of our common ancestors who have committed theft, murder, robberies, rape, to gratify themselves and others. When I open my eyes I feel more at ease. But as soon as I try to sleep, these faces appear again. Unlike old-time specters, they do not lurk in windows or dark corners, they are right inside me. It is my mind that shapes them, being in some mysterious way connected with all the horrors of past centuries and the present. When I bow, after the applause in the concert hall, I'm sometimes aware of these monstrous faces behind every smiling face in the audience. I withdraw into seclusion, and at times, when touching one single key, I succeed in forgetting everything. I see her, Corda, the only blessing granted me in this life — the one you want to take away from me."

"That's not true, Rait, and besides, it seems to me as if you were trying to nonplus me with fabrications of your own. But, really, there must be smoke somewhere . . ."

"There's no smoke, doctor, you imagine it because you're tipsy. Let me pour you some more Burgundy.

"Once, while touring the provinces, I visited a place where I tried to find out about the fate of the parents of an orphan boy, Reinis Garkalns. The boy's mother was said to have died in childbirth, possibly because she had been terribly depressed by her husband's death — he had perished in a fire. Their house had burned down, and it was rumored that Garkalns himself had set fire to it, being a person of a very jealous and passionate nature and suspicious of the young doctor of the district. Anyhow, it had been the work of a madman. He met his death in the conflagration while his wife was saved as if by a miracle. The young doctor had subsequently shown a great interest in the orphan, although — on account of the gossip — he assisted him only in an indirect manner . . .

"It was the doctor, too, who had tried, with the connivance of the management of the orphanage, to prevent the boy from getting to know anything about his parents and childhood. For this reason, his Christian name and surname were changed. Rait Graumanis does not sound too bad, especially for an artist . . .

"But, to return to the subject, it is indeed regrettable that so many people end their lives because of some passion, misunderstanding, or war. Still, if you come to look at the usual process of dying, there isn't anything particularly nice in that either! Is it not so, doctor? Your mind is mature enough to explain the phenomenon of death. A limit must be set on human curiosity and that's why we gradually turn deaf, blind; our memory wears thin; we begin to forget the atrocities committed by our generation, and just continue to exist as neutral beings, not wanted by anybody in particular. But there are much more beautiful ways of perishing . . . Of course, we do not know the very last thing that is going to happen to us, but that's only fair."

159

"Rait, I didn't realize that it had come to this . . . But there's smoke, smoke! You've set fire to the house . . . Come along with me; really, this is absurd! Life always provides us with something to think about. Remember your art, your fame, you are at the summit of your success . . ."

The doctor pulled me by the sleeve toward the door, but the door was locked and I did not know where I had put the key. Perhaps it was in the cellar with the Burgundy.

In the end, he jumped from the window, probably without seriously hurting himself, and probably saving himself for a very dull and undistinguished death which is the fate of people of his kind.

I sat down at the piano and, for a start, struck one single key, wondering how such a wonderful fire could develop from this single sound . . . Then I struck several keys. What strange sounds, how they floated! Corda, my own Corda, was standing by my shoulder, slightly bending forward, like an eternal light of which I did not know the source.

TOYS

LINGER for a while in front of a shop window displaying toys, and you will forget the rest of the world which bothers you: the present, the morrow, clothes and worries, the conflict with others and within yourself.

What strange proportions, what bright colors! A wooden duck, bigger than a whole platoon of tin soldiers; a brown donkey and, astride it, an uncourted doll, with eyes expectant and arms extended; hanging from a trapeze, a little black devil who, as yet, has not harmed anybody; a shiny trumpet for a joyous, as yet unsounded, reveille; a yacht with white sails, waiting for a breeze to carry her to a distant unknown harbor . . . An entire world, transfixed in the moment of creation, which is calling you back to those days when nothing was yet fulfilled and everything seemed a miracle.

You remember that all the toys once given to you have long since been broken or lost. Well, just go into the shop and buy some cheap thing — a rattle decorated with Alpine scenery, cows, lambs, and shepherds. When you turn it you hear a sweet tinkle of bells, a magic sound which chases away all evil. You have heard so many hymns and marches in your life, sounds of victory and despair, that only the tintinnabulation of these small bells can still give you joy. If, at night, you vainly try to find sleep and are tormented by gloomy thoughts,

161

get up and gently shake the rattle; your neighbors won't hear it, or if they do they will wonder at the sounds and think them to be the fluttering of an angel's wings in their dream.

The days of childhood are at once so near and so far that it is only in the dead of night or in complete solitude that you can evoke them. For, with the passing of the years, the hours become ever deeper and the striking of the clock more portentous. Time, the great mystery, rules the human body and mind, and there is no place where one can hide from it. It is useless to try to convince yourself that you are still the same as you were a decade or two ago. But the wonderful continuity of memory makes you at times look at your life as you would look at a smoked golden-scaled fish in the market — from head to tail, as it were: What does it all add up to?

What a strange spring life is mounted upon if the most pitiful of individuals — Johann Vurm, for example, the music teacher on the lower floor — would not even dream of renouncing it in order to be reincarnated as the heir to the British throne, maybe, and forget that he had once been Johann Vurm!

In this respect we are all alike, equally happy and equally pitiful.

A rattle twirled! Here they are: the bygone years, pants and thoughts grown longer, the double and triple change of teeth, the hair gone beyond recall . . . What a quantity of forgotten trigonometrical formulas and historical dates, and nothing left of botany but faded roses. Why all these tribulations? You have sinned, you have treated your toys barbarously!

The usual parental reproach: why do children break their toys so quickly? The inside of the toy automobile taken to pieces on the very first day — why? Well, what sort of car is it if its motor does not even lend itself to investigation? The doll's dress becomes drenched in no time and its colors run; every dress must be washed, a fact so important that it is absolutely impossible to wait until it is sufficiently soiled! Strings of glass beads and the ornaments of the Christmas tree perish as imperceptibly as those childhood days.

162

The paper angel on the silver star at the top of the Christmas tree holds its position to the very last — it is so high up! — while the fir tree itself turns yellow, beginning to shed its needles and changing into something quite incomprehensible — like all pleasures experienced — just good enough to be burnt or thrown away.

The toys that defy their fate longest are generally of the simplest make: a wooden doll whose dress, like her conscience, is unfading and unchangeable, and who neither says "mama" when she is put to bed nor shuts her eyes, for she sleeps open-eyed; a pebble streaked with colored veins and found on some beach — a king to whom God has denied the faculty of speech but who rules all the same, for the child has given him part of its soul; a twisted piece of wood which somehow happens to look like a squirrel.

Complex toys are taken apart for investigation. The simple ones are animated with the complexity of the human soul. To blame the child for breaking them would be out of place. For is it any different in the case of adults? Nature's veils are removed in the search for cause and effect, and the spell is broken. And the Great Donor looks with a pensive smile on this misdeed. The secret of all life's springs is still His. When everything has been investigated and disjoined, we stand with empty hands: won't there be some new presents, some new wonders?

I have seen the birth of a doll; one might say I have been as good as present at the "creation of the world." It was an old man who made the dolls; only old people have so much patience. Onto a wooden model he glued layer after layer of newspaper. When the doll-to-be was dry, the body and limbs were slit open with a knife at the sides and the paper skin peeled off the wooden model; the cuts were then pasted over with more paper, covered with a coat of pink varnish, and the body of the doll was finished.

"Now we must give them a soul," the old man said, and he painted their faces and glued the hair on. These were no factory dolls which all look alike. Their creator treated each one of them individually,

163

adorning their faces with a smile, smiling all the while himself and perhaps remembering the girls he had met in his youth.

The doll-maker was about sixty years old, I was nine, and both of us watched with interest to see what each doll would turn out like. Look! What gorgeous ladies, with a hollow inside, issued from his hands! They were strong and beautiful; however, they were not to be bathed! The daughters of the doll-maker were pretty, too; they could play the piano and dance the mazurka. But that was no help to them in this life. It was 1918, there was chaos and civil war in Russia, and the whole family subsisted at times exclusively on bartering the dolls for food. The daughters lent them their hair; at that time hair was still worn long, and it sufficed for a great number of dolls. Dresses were made for them out of old evening gowns.

One particular doll took my fancy. She looked so sweet and ethereal in her blue silk dress, with her one arm extended as if just waiting for someone to come and ask her for a mazurka. Perhaps her creator, too, was particularly fond of her; the other dolls disappeared quickly, bartered for food and tobacco, while this one remained on the shelf like a marvellous reminder of bygone glory and youth. The doll-maker might have given her to me, who knows; but I dared not ask him.

My parents had rented a couple of rooms in his flat; we saw each other daily, and he was one of the nicest persons I can remember from my childhood. The Christmas toys which had been carefully kept by his daughters had long since passed into my possession — at a period when times did not yet seem so hard. From him you could learn how to build marvellous castles with just colored paper and glue, and also an easy way of making a cigarette hull out of tissue paper. The paper was rolled around a small wooden pin, and a well-rolled mouthpiece of a somewhat stronger paper was plugged with a bit of cotton and inserted into the tissue paper hull before it was stripped off the pin.

Gradually the doll-maker also learned to make shoes out of tar-

164

paulin, canvas, and discarded rubber shoes. Before the revolution he had held a high post in the civil service, and one could only wonder how his hands had acquired the delicate touch and dexterous skill required for making all those useful things.

But I was too shy to ask for the doll. I fully realized that she was no longer a suitable plaything for a boy of my age; besides, when times grew worse, my parents enjoined me not to ask anything of the old gentleman for he was too kindhearted to refuse.

I continued to love her from a distance, daring but rarely to lift her from the shelf and stroke her soft silk dress. We saw each other every day, and this love of mine grew like those in old-time romances of chivalry.

Then, one morning, the doll was no longer there. With a questioning look I gazed at the empty place on the shelf until the old gentleman noticed my expression.

"We gave Liubochka away — yesterday . . ." he said guiltily. We looked at each other for a moment, each measuring the depth of the other's pain. That evening I cried secretly.

That, perhaps, is the reason why I always feel sad about toys. I think I was torn away from them too soon. The moment they began to acquire a deeply human significance, I had to renounce them. It is true, though, that in later years I was given a Monte Cristo pistol and a bicycle, yet secretly I still have a nostalgic longing for Teddy bears and that wonderful doll.

But perhaps mine is not an exceptional case at all. I remember how, one Christmas, I was invited to the home of an author who had bought a toy tank for his six-year-old boy. I arrived before the other guests. We each drank a glass of wine and gave the tank a try. It was a good tank (the author himself had served in a tank regiment), and we sent it back and forth between us and in all directions. It was a treat to see how it overcame the obstacles of the terrain, crawling over the bumps in the carpet. But then it knocked against the foot of the Christmas tree, got entangled in a low branch and —

165

stopped. The tank was broken, the regulator had slid off the spring or perhaps was even broken, and the father — a tank man! — did not know how to repair it. We were rather embarrassed when Christmas Eve came and the tank had to be given to the boy with its motor broken. The expert eye of the young owner noticed it immediately.

A fellow worker of mine once told me how he had vainly tried to gain access to an editor's office just before Christmas. The door had been locked, but from behind it had come strange exclamations and a rumbling noise, then a few incoherent words, then smash, crash, bang! — and laughter.

"Knock harder on the door!" someone had advised him. "The editor is demonstrating to the boss the new toy train he has bought for his son." . . .

In the furnished room where I had been living for a time, the cover of the inkstand had for two years been adorned with a plaster of Paris chicken with a necktie and a cap shaped like the tinfoil cap of a champagne cork. It was a really charming and elegant chicken. Then, one day, it fell and broke its neck. I glued its head on again, and it resumed its place on the inkstand. However, when I looked at the white scar round its neck, I always felt as if I myself had been injured. I knew there are far more things broken in the world than the necks of plaster figurines — in fact, so many that it would be quite impossible to repair them all, even if there were more love than glue in the world. And yet, with the neck, some sound idea may have been broken off and is now pining away inside the little figure's head like a crippled invalid. It may be so, for all I know . . .

Things are broken in the end: one's favorite doll cowers in the corner with a ragged skirt and matted hair; the Teddy bear has his insides taken out and has the emaciated look of a person sick with cancer — even his ears droop.

But the toys that are indestructible are quite simple: pieces of wood or stone, acorns, horse chestnuts — idols and images to whom no harm can come because they have been steeped in human imagi-

166

nation, the warmth of the hearth, and the wonder of the human heart; qualities which are remembered when a plaster of Paris chicken breaks its neck.

I gave away the rattle with the Alpine scenery; it sounded too delicate and dreamy, it was good only for one night. I was afraid I would get too accustomed to it.

I have now taken a fancy to something else. Really, it is a wonderful invention, simple as all ingenious things are: a wooden harlequin, with double-jointed legs, set wide apart. If you stand him on a sloping surface — a board or a book cover — and give him a slight push, he will walk downhill. There he goes, tap-a-tap-tap, tap-a-tap-tap, until he stumbles against the horizontal floor and falls down — bump! One ought to teach him to walk uphill. But that is probably against the laws of nature or mechanics. Toys are just as subject to them as we are.

BEK

MY FATHER loved horses. He was a man of strong feelings but, being a farmer's son, he had a particular, passionate tenderness for horses; it sprang from an inborn responsiveness to nature and all living creatures, and had combined with the skill and knowledge he had gained as an officer of the horse artillery.

One of my early recollections — if not the earliest — is of myself sitting on a horse. My father holds the reins, my mother smiles up at me, and they support me on either side; it is a beautiful summer morning, the road leads through a Russian village, and we slowly advance toward the sun and toward the wide world which I consciously discover for the first time and which bursts upon me like a miracle. There are red thistles growing by the roadside, and everything is steeped in warmth and brightness. I cannot remember whether I was afraid (I certainly was on a later occasion when I was given a ride on a camel).

That moment probably remained unforgettable because of my intense, amazed delight at finding myself so high up and looking down on my parents and the countryside around me. And the thistles! There was a gorge behind the village, completely overgrown with flowering thistles, a fantastically beautiful sight — a dreamlike mythical garden with plants reaching above my head, a place where one could get lost and suddenly take fright at one's loneliness. There are many beautiful sweet-scented flowers in the world, but when I see a red thistle by a roadside I am drawn toward it as though an unrequited love of long ago were calling me.

At that time I was probably two or three years old. It was before the First World War. My father worked as a surveyor, traversing the endless Siberian plains and marking the boundaries of new peasant settlements. My young mind retained a jumble of images, merging into each other, vanishing, re-appearing. I remember herds of wild Siberian horses, small, nimble, tough, shaggy horses, and squint-eyed Kirghiz men and dark-skinned women with necklaces of silver coins. And there were long, drowsy, monotonous rides in horse-drawn vehicles, drives through snowstorms, and drives in the sweltering heat of summer.

I remember the great occasion when I was given mare's milk to drink, a pale sourish liquid which the Kirghiz peasants fermented in leather bags and called "koumis." When my mother noticed some dirt at the bottom of the cup, she would not allow me to finish the milk, and poured the remainder on the ground. Afterwards, my father was very angry with her: she should not have poured the milk out — the Kirghiz who had given us hospitality in his hut was sure to be offended.

Eventually we returned to our own corner of the world. My father had saved some money in order to buy a farm. But the outbreak of war put an end to his plans, and he had to get back into the uniform he had worn in the Russo-Japanese war. After the first battles in Lithuania, which he survived unharmed, he was sent back to the rear and put in charge of a veterinary station. This was quite in keeping with the favorite saying of the artillery: We shoot far, and we are the first to withdraw!

Once more, my attention was focused on horses. Thin, mangy, exhausted, suffering from various ailments, they arrived from the front and had to be nursed back to health. Then they were either re-

169

turned to the front lines or, if considered unfit for further service, sold to the farmers. At times there were up to two thousand horses at the station: cart horses, nags requisitioned from farmers, saddle horses, and thoroughbreds. My father always picked out a few which he kept for riding and driving. But no sooner had they recovered and settled down, no sooner had he befriended them and begun to love them, than they had to be sent back into battle — or they were appropriated by senior officers.

My father had a knack for matching a pair of horses in color, height and pace, and for discovering soldiers who were firstrate drivers with a natural gift for managing horses. As a result, his teams quickly attracted the attention of the officers at the garrison and were snatched away from him. It was always such a wrench to have to part from his favorites that my father decided to buy some horses for his own use and to place them in private stables. This could be done with a little cunning: the horses had to be chosen while they were still a sorry sight and nobody wanted them; shabby and ill, they could easily be included among the lot that was for sale.

Thus it came about that for the first and only time in my life I had a horse of my own: Grieta, a white mare of rather melancholy disposition. She was no longer in her first youth, but she had once been a famous trotter and had won prizes at the Riga hippodrome. My parents had long before decided that I should have riding lessons, but it was winter, and my lessons had to be postponed till the spring. Meanwhile, the only outlet I had for my feelings of ownership was to offer Grieta pieces of bread which she accepted readily enough; but, on the whole, her attitude toward me was rather one of condescension, and her affability went no further than to eating what I brought her. She had doubtless seen many a fine gentleman in her time, and I could hardly hope to impress her — I could merely astonish her with my small stature.

But a much greater event was about to take place. One evening my father came home very much excited; for a long time he paced up and down the room with jingling spurs, and I heard a large sum of money being mentioned as he talked to my mother. I was not consulted, of course, but I gathered what it was all about. A cavalry officer, just back from the front, had been unlucky at cards and had contracted serious debts; he now had to sell his horse. It was not easy for him to part with it, and he was anxious to find a buyer who would recognize its true merits and give it all the care it deserved. It probably cost my father half the money he had saved up for the farm, but he never had cause to regret it.

The horse was Bek, a white Arab, daintily dappled with brown and black, and with a coat so fine that one could see the veins underneath. True, he was rather thin, but oats and proper care soon set that right. When he appeared in the yard, strutting and prancing, with his flowing white mane and with his tail reaching down to the ground, he looked exactly like the horses of the heroes in my books of fairy tales. When I offered him a lump of sugar he picked it up so carefully that his lips barely touched my palm, and he gave me a friendly, altogether human look. No, this horse wasn't like Grieta who took everything I gave her and never even bothered to look at me. Here was courtesy, here was a superior intelligence! From that moment, I regarded Bek as my great friend.

Toward spring I often managed to steal unobserved into the stable and bring him gifts of bread and sugar; I stroked his velvety lower lip and scratched him under the chin, which he liked because it was a place he could not reach himself. In fact, I stroked him all over; I studied the pattern of his coat, fondled his smooth tail, and crawled beneath his belly across to his other side — an action he watched with polite curiosity, no doubt wondering how it could possibly give anyone pleasure. I paid no attention when the grownups warned me to be careful, and I felt just as safe by his tail as by his head. It was quite unthinkable that Bek should ever want to kick me, and warnings that he might seemed a calumny of my very good friend's character. As if it were likely that he had ever tried to kick any-

171

body! When he had visitors he never flicked back his ears irritably as the other horses did when something annoyed them; like a real gentleman, attentively, pleasantly, he always looked straight into the eyes of the person with whom he was concerned.

Now, in retrospect, I tend to think that I must often have been a great nuisance to Bek; my visits to him were certainly far more numerous than was known to my parents or the day laborers who cleaned the stable. On only one occasion did he wrong me. Perhaps, from his own point of view, it was no misdeed but simply the most careful chastisement such a large creature could possibly deal out to a little fellow like me.

It happened in the summer. Bek stood by the tethering post in the yard. We were alone and, as usual, I produced a lump of sugar as a preliminary to our conversation. Perhaps he had expected something more, or perhaps my attentions had begun to bore him. Be that as it may, he suddenly gripped the tip of my middle finger between his teeth when I tickled his lower lip. He gripped it and would not let go. My finger hurt. Of course, he could easily have bitten it off. But he clearly had no such intention; he merely held my finger so firmly that I could not pull it away, and he regarded me with his usual expression, friendly, slightly mocking. This situation continued unbearably long. "Bek!" I entreated, "Let go, do let go!" I began to cry, I pounded his nose with my other hand, but he did not relent.

At last, when I was quite in despair and my cheeks were streaming with tears, Bek released my finger. I rushed away to have a look at it; there was a nasty bruise like a large inkstain, the blood had come to the surface under the skin. I cried again, and at first I wanted to run and complain to my mother. But something held me back. I felt that this matter had to be settled between Bek and myself alone, and I did not show my finger to anyone.

The bruise gradually turned all the colors of the rainbow and finally black and grey; meanwhile I tormented myself with conjec-

172

tures as to why Bek had done this to me. If Grieta had done it, or Guna — my mother's dapple-grey mare — it wouldn't have surprised me, and I would have been quick to complain about it to my parents. But Bek was my best friend — and suddenly he had done such a thing! I kept away from him for several days, but I felt his eyes watching my every movement and knew that he pricked up his ears and turned his head to see where I was going.

In time, we made it up. Actually, there was no need for a reconciliation as far as he was concerned. He was the same as he had always been — an affable, highly sensitive Arab to whom a little boy's love could not really matter very much. But he never showed that this was so. Neither did I ever see him display anger. Even the yard man's dog, always yapping and barking, did not get much response from Bek; the horse merely tossed his head and raised his foreleg as though to say: "Goodness me, why all this fuss? Can't you do anything but bark?"

After riding, the horses were walked about in the yard for half an hour until they cooled off. Usually this was the job of the day laborers, but I was allowed to take charge of Bek. Sometimes the two of us, deep in conversation, oblivious of the passing of time, kept on walking until darkness fell; I never had to tug at the bridle when we came to the corners of the yard — he knew perfectly well that he was to walk in a circle.

My riding lessons had begun, and I had already been put on Grieta's back a few times. It seemed a terribly high perch to me. The most difficult thing of all was to climb up there without assistance. On these occasions, though, Grieta displayed her excellent qualities. She stood perfectly still, quite unperturbed by my fumblings and clamberings along her side. If I accidentally dropped the reins as she was slowly pacing along, she would stop and wait while I groped under her neck to retrieve them.

Yet I did not enjoy those first attempts at riding for I was thwarted in my thirst for glory. The trouble was that I had a Cossack saddle,

173

high and heavy, with all sorts of contraptions dangling from it; the front of it came up in a high arch convenient to grip in an emergency. It was the kind of saddle used for long cross-country rides, and my father had once laughingly remarked that no great skill was required to keep one's seat in a thing like that. Ever since he'd said that, I had coveted an English saddle — light, flat, and giving practically no support, so that everything depended on the rider's leg muscles.

Then I got such a saddle, smaller than for adults, and specially ordered for me. It arrived one morning, and I could not bear to wait; I put it on a stool and tried it out. Yes, it was marvellous to ride like that — in the room! But when the saddle was placed on Grieta's broad back the art of riding immediately presented new snares and difficulties. Many a time I had to grit my teeth and fight back my tears, for my family disapproved of crying.

After a few months I was able to canter up and down the broad avenue in front of the house, rising in the stirrups in the rhythm of Grieta's movements, and exhilarated by the day laborer's shouts of approval. He was a cavalryman, a Latvian named Engelis, which means Angel. And, indeed, his patience was angelic.

My father, however, had a very different temperament, and there were rather stormy scenes in the course of my riding lessons. I had to learn to sit in the saddle just right, neither too stiff nor too slack, and hold the reins in such a way that the horse did not have its neck forced back and yet was made to feel who was master. And it was not enough merely to learn all these things — one had to acquire an instinctive knowledge, one had to feel it in one's very bones if anything was wrong. It was Engelis's job to accompany me on another horse when I went riding, and this took place every morning at precisely nine o'clock. Later, he confined himself to standing by the gate and watching me canter up and down the avenue. As time went on, his appearances became rarer, and I reached the summit of blissful pride when he no longer showed himself by the gate at all.

Grieta habitually broke into an easy canter, swift and rhythmical.

174

On only a few exceptional occasions could she be persuaded to break into a gallop. Usually she continued with her canter when the other horses were already going at a gallop, and yet she did not fall behind. But she could not keep pace with Bek, of course. It really was a sight worth seeing when my father took it into his head to give him full rein. His tail streaming in the wind, Bek straightened out like an arrow shot from a bow: horse and rider merged into one single being, careering across fields and ditches as though to hurl themselves into perdition. After such an experience it always took Bek a long time to calm down; he excitedly tossed his dainty little head, his rosy nostrils dilated and contracted, and there was an air of achievement about him for he had fulfilled his true function in life: to be swift and beautiful. How different this was from accepting lumps of sugar from a small boy's hand and letting oneself be led around the yard! At such times I felt acutely that I was still only a child, whereas Bek was grown up and complete. Now and then I was allowed to ride him slowly in the yard, and he put up with it. In general, though, my father did not like anyone to ride Bek, not even the day laborer. There were subtle modes of communication between my father and Bek, which might have been interrupted by the intrusion of another rider.

With Grieta, it was quite a different matter; but unfortunately she ruined my good name as a rider. Goodness knows how she had discovered that no great effort was needed to dislodge me from the saddle. She acquired a habit of suddenly stopping between two paces and jerking her head downwards — and I went hurtling through the air, obeying the primary rule of all good cavalrymen: Don't get your feet entangled in the stirrups when you feel the fight is lost!

Grieta stood there and turned her head, curious to see what was happening to me, waiting peacefully until I climbed back into the saddle. To do her justice, I must add that she never played such tricks during a fast canter but reserved them for leisurely moments when I had slackened the reins and she could catch me off my guard.

175

One day she threw me three times. Oh yes, I had become a source of amusement to lighten her old age! And there was nothing I could do about it, even though I possessed an elegant bamboo cane with a leather loop at the end, all in accordance with the rules of superior riding establishments. She quite simply did not take me seriously.

To give Grieta time to forget her antics, I was allowed to ride a well-trained cavalry horse, a sorrel. But he played a devilish trick which almost proved fatal to me; it certainly was worse than all the pranks Grieta could possibly think of. The sorrel came from the army stables, and he must have taken a great fancy to something there: one day, as we happened to be in their neighborhood, he suddenly darted off toward them at frantic speed, flatly refusing to obey the reins. I was not strong enough to curb the mad gallop of such a powerful brute; all I could do was hold on and watch the low stable doors approaching at terrifying speed. They had been left open, there was not a single soldier to be seen anywhere, and it was most unlikely that the horse would spare any thought for my life and limbs as he careered through the doors. But Engelis saved me. Riding after me, he overtook me on the little bridge before the stables, snached the reins from my hands, and managed to control both horses. To tell the truth, I had not realized the full extent of my danger; it was the grownups who got the biggest fright.

Winter came. I had to interrupt my riding, putting an end to such joys and misadventures. Toward spring, Grieta gave birth to a filly. Guna's foal, named Indulis, had been born a month before, but its entry into the world did not impress me half so much as its subsequent pranks. The birth of Grieta's filly, however, was an event of consequence; in this case I was the unquestionable owner. It was a dainty, fragile little creature, light brown, with long spindly legs and with a white star on its forehead. Still damp, and trembling a little, it crawled out from beneath the blanket and unerringly made its way to its mother's milk. I had never seen such a tiny little horse, and such a beautiful one. We named it Ariya. But, as with Grieta,

I could not establish any friendly relation with the filly. It was highly sensitive and capricious, shy and reserved, and it did not like people to touch it. Indulis, on the other hand, became everybody's favorite; he soon developed into quite a rascal. Both foals were beautiful, and one could see at a glance that Bek's noble blood ran in their veins. Indulis was the darker of the two, with an alert, mischievously determined look. He was afraid of nothing.

Having discovered that people usually had bread in their pockets when they came to see him, Indulis speedily conceived the idea of looking for it there. If he did not find any bread he stood up on his hindlegs and put his forelegs on his visitor's shoulders. This was a game that delighted him — and it was all right as far as the grownups were concerned. But the snag was that he grew faster than I did. As he became bigger he convinced himself soon enough that he was stronger than I. Several times he pushed me over when he put his forelegs on my shoulders. He clearly had the upper hand, and he enjoyed this so much that sometimes, catching sight of me, he made a wild dash at me — with the object of knocking me over.

In fact, he began to persecute me. To get out into the road, we had to cross the yard, and I was reduced to peeping cautiously round the front door of the house to see whether Indulis was sufficiently far away in the yard so that I could safely dart across to the gate. He was lying in wait for me when I came home, too. Once he did not even hesitate to follow me up a few steps of the porch. It became a daily occurrence to see his head suddenly appear through the open window of the ground floor kitchen. He examined all the dishes within his reach, salads and cucumbers had to be whisked away quickly, and even stewed fruit tickled his fancy.

His favorite pastime in the yard was chasing the hens and pigeons. Even the big cock who usually never lost his dignity and, when frightened, used merely to retreat sideways in the wake of his wives, uneasily cackling — even he, when pursued by Indulis, fled helter-skelter, his neck outstretched, with never a sound.

177

When we went for a drive, with Guna between the shafts, Indulis ought to have trotted peacefully beside her as befits a well-bred foal. Instead, he cantered away, keeping about a hundred paces ahead, chasing after all living creation — geese, hens, and pigs — making a straight dash at dogs, shaking little children by the scruff of their necks, and attacking even the old women who had been gathering berries and mushrooms in the wood. Several times my father had to pay for the strawberries spilled out of the women's baskets, and things generally got so much out of hand that the reckless creature had to be put into the army stables to learn some manners. Later he was sold to a horse trainer. I saw him again when he was already a yearling; at the end of a long rope, he was learning to run in a circle. Indulis had outgrown his childhood pranks, he seemed very big and grave, and he no longer remembered me.

Bek also was no longer among us. When he died in the summer, my father suspected that he had been poisoned. Russia was plunged into confusion and disorder, and relations had become strained between the officers and the soldiers who cleaned the stables. The veterinary surgeon was unable to diagnose Bek's illness. For hours, the horse was walked about in the yard. Watching from the window, I saw Bek, clearly in great pain, obediently, doggedly pacing along. His flanks were wet with perspiration, his head hung listlessly, and he raised his beautiful legs with a dull, monotonous movement as though performing a wearisome duty. At nightfall, his white body lay motionless in the yard. I was not allowed to go out and look at him. The day laborer told me that my father had refused to have the horse flayed although there was a buyer who wanted the hide. Bek was secretly buried outside the town. At home, everybody went about in gloomy silence as though one of the family had died. It was torture to have to exchange a few words of conversation, and my father did not join us at meals for several days.

For the first time in my life I had lost something that had never tangibly belonged to me, and yet I grieved more than I had ever done when I lost a toy or got a scolding from my parents. It was a great sorrow, and it filled my room from wall to wall, permeating my whole being and my small childhood world. It was so great that no tears could mitigate it. For the first time it dawned upon me that things happen in life which should not happen and yet have an undisputed place in the pattern of human existence.

Soon afterwards, my father left the army; we moved into a smaller house and sold the remaining horses, but this made no particular impression on me. There were new events and new interests; preoccupied with them, I did not notice that something was slipping away never to return.

DATE DUE